6.48

BRETT RANDALL, GAMBLER

Lary Day escaped from the law and watched another man accidentally die in his place . . . a man who was his exact double! He had the choice of running away and living a fugitive's life—or of assuming the dead man's place. Every clue pointed to the dead man being the real murderer . . . but proving it meant becoming just as crooked and ruthless as Gary Elliot had been. No matter what Lary decided he was bound to end up dead!

E. B. MANN

BRETT RANDALL, GAMBLER

Complete and Unabridged

LINFORD
Leicester

Originally published as Thirsty Range

First Linford Edition
published July 1988

Copyright © 1935 by E. B. Mann
All rights reserved

British Library CIP Data

Mann, E. B.
 Brett Randall, gambler.—Large print ed.—
Linford western library
 I. Title
 813'.52[F]

ISBN 0-7089-6527-X

Published by
F. A. Thorpe (Publishing) Ltd.
Anstey, Leicestershire
Set by Rowland Phototypesetting Ltd.
Bury St. Edmunds, Suffolk
Printed and bound in Great Britain by
T. J. Press (Padstow) Ltd., Padstow, Cornwall

1

LARY DAY set first one boot and then the other upon the bottom rail of the corral fence, bending twice to test the solidity of the spurs that jutted stiffly from his heels. These were old boots, soft and worn and vastly comfortable after the hot pressure of the new and shiny ones they had replaced.

In the chute a little distance to his left, two helpers cursed listlessly as they set a bucking shell upon a horsehide full of dynamite. The horse lunged wickedly as the cinch came snug against his ribs so that the smash and rattle of the gate rang like a challenge through the smokey heat. A man laughed nervously.

"You better fork him, Day," he called. "Looks like he ain't a-gonna wait!"

Day stood erect and grinned. "If he's in a hurry, let him go," he said. "A man can always catch a later train."

He turned and watched a tall, blue-shirted man swing up and settle gingerly upon a hump-back sorrel mare. The announcer's voice blared through the giant megaphone and rebounded from the stands: "Danny Lightfoot, ladies and gents; Danny Lightfoot, comin' up on Sulky Sue in the finals for the men's bronc ridin' championship. Watch him, folks! Danny Lightfoot, on Sulky Sue, in the arena!"

Beyond the tense, still group in the arena the grandstands made a high, banked curve against the sky. The sorrel mare lunged back impatiently, striking up with both forefeet across the neck of a helper's mount. A man swore curtly and eared her down again. A wave of sound flowed through the stands, a gusty sigh. Day thought, "There's forty thousand people there; and yet, on Sue, he'll be alone, the same as in another world."

Pop Greer spoke quietly from Lary's left, "In just about ten minutes now you'll be the champeen bronc twister of the world. I ain't so sure I ought to speak to you!"

He was a gnarled, bow-legged little man, incongruous beside Day's spare six feet of height. He peered up anxiously, blue eyes almost devoid of color by contrast with the weathered tan of the surrounding skin, his thin down-curving mustache twitching oddly as he searched Day's face for signs of strain. Day grinned as he glanced down at Greer.

"Either that or a dirty deuce out of a dog-eared pack," he said. "Sue's tough, and Danny'll made a pretty ride."

"He's good, that Indian," Pop Greer agreed. "But he's careful. He'll made a tight, hard ride. And you'll ride by the seat of your pants, like you always do. Besides, you've got a tougher horse."

"There he goes!"

Lightfoot's clear voice cracked out into the hush, shrill and jubilant as waiting ended in the sharp relief of conflict. "Turn 'er loose!" The group in the arena split apart, the helping riders wheeling hastily as Lightfoot whipped the blindfold off Sue's head. The sorrel mare exploded in a twisting leap. The rider's head snapped back.

Day turned away. He had no desire to burden his own mind just then with the perfection of the Indian's skill. The swelling roar from the stands beat in his ears. He climbed the sidewall of the chute and straddled it, feeling the heavy timbers strain as the black beast inside came hard against the wall. To the west, beyond the park, the russet ridges stretched endlessly into a thin blue haze where they met the sky. Beyond that veil, the peaks thrust up to form the backbone of the world. "It's cool up there," Day thought. "This is a rotten job."

A gunshot cut the surf-like din and Lary turned in time to see the Indian vault into the clear across a helper's mount. The Sue mare whipped away, still bucking. A man beside the chute gate said, "He made a straight-up ride. I bet his belly aches!"

The uproar in the stands swelled higher still as Lightfoot turned to leave the field. He walked stiffly, weaving a little, his stoic face a little drawn. Blood ran from his nose in two thin lines that curved along the grooves set in his face by rigid lips. He glanced at Lary as he passed and raised one hand. Day lifted both hands head-high, right fist in his open palm, congratulating him. The roar died down. The crowd sat back, awaiting other thrills.

The voice from the megaphone beat through the last hoarse murmurings. "And now, ladies and gents—Lary Day, on Hellamile, Chute Number Three! You know him, folks. You know 'em both! And here they come!"

Lary Day stood up. Two men bore down on Pop Greer and paused to speak to him. Pop answered them and both men turned to stare at Day. A silver star gleamed brightly on a whipcord vest and Lary frowned. "I'm in the money now," he thought, "and somebody's figurin' to collect a cut of it."

He swung one leg across the chute, straddling it. A girl on a palomino mare went past him, single-footing, and Lary met her friendly gaze. She reined up sharply, astonishment replacing casual interest in her face. Day smiled and saw her lips move slowly, seemingly to frame his name. Her face was oval, olive tanned, with firm red lips and eyes more darkly blue than any Day had ever seen. Her hair, the bit of it that he could see beneath her broad-rimmed hat, was bright ash blonde, the color of valley mist when slanting sunlight touches it with gold. She wheeled toward him and he saw the blue contestant's card pinned to her shirt. The palomino wore no brand but there was a Bar 11 burned into the corner of the saddle skirt.

The black horse in the chute squealed viciously and lashed out with both hind feet against the planks. The palomino shied and reared, the yellow body flashing in the sun. Day waited, watching the girl, liking the long clean lines of leg and back displayed as she sat out the mare's sham fright, liking the caressing movement of her hand against the snowy mane once she had eased the palomino down.

"Why, Gary! Why the masquerade?" And then, accusingly, "You don't remember me!"

Her voice was low, yet with a vibrant quality that made Day think of bells, bronze bells, sweet-toned and clear.

"I don't," he said. "Which proves—"

He would have said, "Which proves I never saw you before in all my life." But she cut in before the words were out.

"Which proves the fickleness of men, Gary! It was the night before you went away to school. You were fifteen and quite grown up! You kissed me, too!"

Her eyes laughed up at him, enjoying his discomfiture. "It was a rather condescending kiss, I remember. After all, I was just thirteen and much beneath your manly dignity . . . It isn't very flattering that you've forgotten it."

The man at the chute gate said, "They're waitin' for you, Day. Get set."

Day did not move. "You're makin' a mistake," he said. "You called me Gary, didn't you? My name is Lary. Lary Day."

He watched the laughter wash out of her eyes to be replaced by doubt, bewilderment. He thought, "When I was fifteen, I was *through* with school!" He shrugged and let his weight down on the bucking shell. The hard, bunched body under him cringed down a little, shuddering. Day thought, "You hate me, don't you, boy? Well, I ain't blamin' you. You're trapped and I'm your enemy. I know just how you feel."

He glimpsed the palomino's head close to the chute and glanced up sidelong through the bars. The girl smiled through at him. "You needn't look so shocked," she said. "I'm not a forward hussy who goes around accosting strange young men; not usually. I really did mistake you for a man I know."

He grinned. "I wasn't shocked. Just envious!"

She laughed and reined the mare away. "Good luck!" she said.

The man outside the chute spoke up again, impatiently. "You ready, Day?"

Day set himself and faced the gate. "And waitin', mister. Turn him loose!"

The gate swung back. The helper leaped aside. The black horse lunged ahead, three long back-snapping jumps, the saddle rocking on the apex of his gabled spine. Day weathered it, his muscles feeling for a rhythm in the hurricane.

The horse dropped sideways and spun, his black mane flattened by the wrenching turn. He shot aloft, back arched to a thin peak beneath the bucking shell; came down to strike unevenly in two side-slipping jolts. Then up again.

Dust swirled around the pounding hoofs to form a low grey fog that cut the man aloof from earth, from all reality. He sat marooned up on a high and lonely seat, a seat that smashed his spine into his skull with cruel blows. The sunlight faded to a red-streaked blur. The horse sunfished and weaved, swapped ends; but always when he struck it was upon pile-driving, rigid legs through which the shock ran up straight to the rider's brain.

An evil snakelike head came up before Day's eyes and he beat at it with his fist, sledging the black horse down again. The jolt of that descent shot molten pain through Lary's veins. But it was better than the backward fall the horse had planned. He felt his spur wheels rake from neck to flank and knew that he was riding loose and gallantly. "But not for long!" he thought. "Why don't they fire that gun?"

The bucker screamed and went aloft again, his body twisting till the saddle leather creaked. They came above the fog of dust and seemed to hang suspended for a time, the black horse writhing till his forefeet paralleled the ground. Day thought, "He'll never straighten out of this!" And then the forward plunge snapped at his neck.

He felt the sledging impact as the forefeet struck and after that a sickening forward drop. He lost the feel of contact then; struck heavily and rolled. A gunshot cut across his consciousness with mocking tardiness.

He found his feet and staggered up, swaying stubbornly against a seasick world. A rod away the black horse grunted and lurched up, stood motionless, still dazed. Day grinned and tasted blood deep in his throat. A pickup man flung down beside him and reached out to steady him.

"You all right, Day?"

"Okay. I hope the black ain't hurt."

"God damn!" The helper's oath was reverent. "That devil bucked himself clean off his feet! I ain't seen nary ride like that since Steamboat used t' buck 'em down up at Cheyenne!"

Day bent and slapped his hat against his legs.

He was conscious now for the first time of the surflike roar of voices from the stands. He straightened, grinned and made a little shrugging gesture with his hands.

He turned and walked unsteadily toward the chutes. His stomach was a leaden ball, white hot beneath his ribs. His legs were numb. He thought, "A man's a fool to take that kind of punishment. . . . That black can pitch!"

He walked straight into Pop Greer's arms. The old man's voice cut through the fog that veiled his consciousness. "You all right, son?"

"Sure, Pop. Just pounded some. I landed light."

He blinked and stared at Greer's grave face. There was trouble there; a trouble unrelieved by Lary's words. He said, "Cheer up! Hell, second money ain't so bad! . . ."

Behind Pop Greer a silver star caught sunlight like a gem and Day looked past the old man's hat into a pair of steel-grey eyes. A vague foreboding tugged at nerves already taut.

"I'm Blaine, the sheriff here. Ed Brown, my deputy . . . You're Lary Day?" The rising tone was challenging.

"So what?" Day said.

"I hate to do it, Day. You made a pretty ride out there." Blaine shrugged and frowned. "You're wanted, see? You'll have to come with me."

Somewhere in the distance the hoarse excitement of the crowd reechoed like a distant cannonade. Nearby a steer bawled lustily. But here was silence like a deathbed hush. Day saw Blaine's hand slide down toward a holstered gun. He thought, "This thing is serious. He wouldn't be on edge like this about a minor thing." He drove his mind into his recent past in search of clues; found none.

A man ran past the corner of the horse corral just back of Blaine and Day's eyes shifted instantly. The runner halted, feet widespread, his right arm bowed so that his hand poised, talonlike, above a gun. He was a slender man, no bigger than Pop Greer, but he was dangerous. His eyes were hard and glittering. His face twitched oddly, the slack mouth ugly and malevolent. But as his eyes met Day's the twitching ceased. He licked his lips.

It ran in Lary's mind that here was something taken from a moving picture show. If Blaine turned now, the little man would draw. It would be a shootout, man to man, as in the bad old days. Day wondered what the old man's grievance was. He said, "Stand steady, Blaine. Don't turn around. I'll talk to him."

The look of blank astonishment on Blaine's long face was ludicrous. Day stepped past Blaine and thrust himself between the two of them. But as he moved Blaine wheeled. Day saw the little man's right hand dart down. He yelled, "Don't shoot, you fool!" The shot cracked out.

A smashing blow stopped Day dead in his tracks and thrust him back upon his heels. He saw the gun buck up in hard recoil, a thin blue coil of smoke sliding lazily up past the old man's hat. The man's thin lips writhed back in a derisive grin. Day thought, "He shot at me, not Blaine!" The fact struck into him with paralyzing force.

A yellow horse flashed into view behind the little man, a rider bending wide, one arm aloft. But Lary paid no heed to that. He stood erect, swaying almost imperceptibly, his eyes fixed on that uplifted gun. "I thought that he was after Blaine. I didn't think he'd shoot at me. He must be crazy; run amuck! Somebody ought to knock him down."

He took a step ahead but his legs seemed

rooted to the ground. The gun was coming down again. He heard Blaine's vivid oath. A body struck against Day's hips and Pop Greer's wiry arms encircled him. They went down together, but as they fell Day saw a thin tight loop flip down across the madman's face and jerk him back. The second shot streaked up, unaimed. The yellow horse was backing now, expertly taking up the slack in the thin rope that tied him to a sprawling, squalling thing upon the ground.

Blaine closed the distance in four mighty strides and dropped to pin the little man beneath his weight. Above the swirl of dust their bodies made Day could see the girl who had mistaken him for someone else a while ago. Her face was paler now. "She's scared," he thought. "But not so scared but what she put her string right where it did the most damn good!"

Blaine said, "I've got him now," and tossed the rope-end free. Pop Greer sat up and peered at Day.

"You all right, kid?"

Day nodded and sat up. His left shoulder throbbed numbly and he rubbed it gently with his right hand. His shirt was sticky-wet. His hand was red when it came down. He stared at it. "Seems like I'm nicked," he said.

Pop growled at him. "It's lucky you ain't dead the way you bellied up to him! What's wrong with you? No sabe 'guns'? All I could do was tackle you. He would've got you sure, the second time."

Day heard Blaine's voice directed at the girl. "That was a real neat job. Quick thinkin', too. How did you happen into this?"

The girl's voice was low, a little shaken now. "I saw him running. Something in the way he looked—I knew that there was something wrong. I followed him. But it wasn't until after he fired that first shot that I realized that he was—mad."

Blaine stood up. The little man was quiet now, a huddled gargoyle on the ground, his head bent down above his knees. "He ain't exactly mad," Blaine said. "Leastways, not the way you mean. He knew exactly what he aimed to do, and why."

Day stood up, his left arm limp. He felt a little sick. He stared at Blaine. "You say he knew just what he aimed to do," he said slowly. "You mean he aimed to murder me?"

There was a different look in Blaine's eyes as

he looked into Day's this time; a bleakness and an utter lack of friendliness. "Murder? Well, some folks might have another name for it . . . considerin' what you did to him."

Again there was a tense, electric hush before Day spoke. He said, "I never saw the man before. What did I do to him?"

Blaine shrugged. "There's no use lyin', Day. This man comes in and makes a charge. I came out here to take you in to be identified. I figure then there might be some mistake. The old man followed me out here. One peep at you, he shucks his gun. I reckon he's identified you, right enough. Your goose is cooked."

"And what's the charge?" Day's voice was low.

"The charge is murder, Day," Blaine said. "This man's the father of the girl you killed."

2

LARY DAY sat motionless in the sticky heat of the Sedalia courtroom, his eyes half closed in weary contemplation of his boot toes stretched a long leg's length in front of him. These were the new boots, part of his rodeo gear, which he had taken off before he mounted Hellamile that day; but they were weeks old now and adjusted to his feet. This thing had taken time.

He had discounted it at first, accepting the arrest and the discomforts of imprisonment as parts of some unpleasant error that would soon be rectified. Now, after six long weeks, he was less sure. The evidence was strong, conclusive on the face of it, each bit dovetailed amazingly into the whole.

There was the little old stoop-shouldered man who had so convincingly identified the prisoner at the moment of the arrest: Lafe Turner, father of Belle Turner, who was dead. And there was Mary Ware, Belle Turner's onetime roommate in a San Francisco boarding house, brought here to testify.

"That's him," she said, on oath. "He called himself Ed Rogers then but that's the man."

And there was Joe Blake, hotel night clerk, who testified reluctantly that Lary Day had visited Belle Turner's room the night before she was found dead, her skull crushed in.

Damning testimony, all of it. The night clerk writhed unhappily beneath a scathing cross-examination aimed to slur the character of a hotel in which a man's visit to a lone girl's room might go unquestioned regardless of the length of his stay; for Blake admitted that he had not seen the caller leave. "Testimony to the witness' own detriment," as the State's Attorney pointed out most carefully and thereby won a point.

"And they're sincere!" That fact had slowly beaten into Lary's consciousness. "Doggone it, Pop, those people think they're right!"

Lafe Turner's hatred was an ugly thing, whole-souled and horrible. Day after day, in court, the little man sat motionless, bent forward in his chair, his glittering gaze fixed balefully upon the prisoner, alive with hate. Once Lary saw the old man smile and lick his lips. That sight made Day a little sick.

And Mary Ware, and Blake. "They're tellin' what they honestly believe to be the truth. *I* know it; you can bet the jury does!"

Pop Greer had tried to comfort him. "But hell, they're wrong. We both know it. They're just mistakin' you for someone else."

Day closed his eyes. The State's Attorney was busy now with the final summing up. His voice, suave, confident, ran on and on in Lary's ears.

". . . and it was there in San Francisco that Belle Turner met this man who called himself Ed Rogers. Remember, she was poor; an orphan, far from home, unschooled and innocent. To her, this man with money, flashy clothes and sleek good looks may well have seemed the fairy prince out of some childhood story book. She fell in love with him.

"You have heard the desperate efforts of the Defense to slur this girl's good name; to brand her love a light, unworthy thing. There is no evidence of that; no cause for it except the desperate need of the Defense to find some meager ground for sympathy. The evidence points plainly to the fact. This man seduced that girl; betrayed her innocence and brought her down to shame!

"Perhaps he promised her his name. Perhaps

her love for him was great enough so that she asked not even that. It doesn't matter now. But then she found herself with child. And then, and not till then, did she demand that he protect her name.

"That he refused is obvious from evidence. Her roommate told you how Belle Turner suffered; how she wept and pleaded with him. At last she must have threatened him. She knew him now, remember. She told her roommate that she had discovered his real name. But even then she would not betray him. She never told Mary Ware what she had discovered, nor would she tell her own father. Lafe Turner had visited her, you remember, soon after she first met this man. Lafe Turner saw Ed Rogers many times and warned his girl against the man. So Belle Turner kept her secret from the old man now and fought it out alone, preferring that to what she knew her father would have done.

". . . He wrote to her at last and promised that he'd marry her. Mary Ware has told you how happy Belle Turner was. She was to meet him here, in Sedalia. They would be married here, he said.

"Why he chose this town to be the scene of the crime is obvious. Perhaps his money had run short. At any rate, he meant to take part in the rodeo. It was convenient that she should come to him. Then, too, he must have reasoned that his chances here were better than they would have been where she was known. A stranger, frightened and alone, would be an easy prey.

"But even then he blundered. Perhaps he failed to consider the fact that he was far too good a rider to remain unknown. He could not know that the clerk in the hotel in which Belle Turner stayed was an enthusiastic rodeo fan. He hoped that he would not be recognized.

"And so he killed her, gentlemen. There is no question now but what he planned to do just that when he invited her to come. He took the weapon with him to her room and he took it with him when he left. Just what that weapon was, we do not know. Perhaps it was a gun. 'A heavy, blunted instrument,' no matter what. He smashed her skull with it and then climbed through a window to a fire escape.

"We must admire his nerve, at least. He did not run. He knew that flight would seal his guilt. Instead he made a splendid ride next day on Hellamile that nearly won the championship!"

For six long days the juggernaut of law had lumbered on, grinding the case beneath its wheels to squeeze from it the last thin juice of fact; a grim, slow juggernaut whose clatter beat and tore at Lary's nerves. The solemn rituals, the petty skirmishes and bickerings. . . .

"Your Honor, I object! . . . Objection overruled . . . Look at the defendant. Is that the man? . . . Object! . . . Sustained . . . Face the jury, please . . . Your Honor, what the witness thought cannot be evidence! . . . Answer the question . . . Where were you the night of July third? . . . She told me he promised to meet her here . . . Your Honor, I propose to connect this question later on . . . Objection overruled . . . Exception . . . Answer yes or no."

The Prosecutor's voice went on unceasingly. Day thought, "You're wastin' time. Sit down!" There was no need for oratory now. The case was clinched.

It was amusing, in a way, that all their cleverness and bickering had led them wrong. "The joke's on them," he thought, and smiled a little, savoring the grim wry flavor of the jest. "The trouble is, nobody sees the point but me!"

He shut his ears against the courtroom

sounds and let his mind go back to the beginning of this tragic farce. The scene came back to him: the stands, a seething riot of discordant sound. Danny Lightfoot, walking unsteadily through slanting sunlight, blood curving past his rigid lips.

"I'd never heard of all these people then," Day thought. "I remember thinkin' when I saw Blaine speak to Pop, that he was there to try to make me pay some faked-up debt. They did that to Red Bullard once; caught him just as he came in after a winnin' ride and attached his prize money to pay a hotel bill."

He remembered how Bullard had cursed. One item on that bill had been for eighteen packages of perfumed cigarettes, "I knowed I had to pay it when I seen that," Red had explained. "I'm married, and I smoke a pipe!"

His mind came back to that scene out there beside the bucking chute, to the girl on the yellow mare. She, too, had mistaken him for someone else and only yesterday it had occurred to him to find a glimmering of hope in that coincidence. He remembered how the sun had glistened on her hair and how her nose had crinkled oddly when she laughed. Gary, she had called him. Odd that twice within a day people should mistake him for another man. And yet he gathered that this Gary was a man she had not seen since he had kissed her, years ago.

"She's twenty-one or so," he thought. "And she was thirteen then. Eight years ago. He might not look like me at all by now."

Well, it was just a chance, a meager one. He had spoken to Blaine about it and Blaine had promised to investigate. Her name was Starr Landerson. Blaine had told him that.

"Matt Landerson was her dad," Blaine had explained. "They own a spread down Coronado way. She was up here visitin' the Morgan girls. She went to school with one of them."

"She had a card," Day had remarked, remembering the contestant's card that she had worn pinned to her shirt.

"I reckon Morgan got her that. Morgan backed the show. That card would give her freedom of the grounds." Blaine had laughed and added whimsically, "She might've entered for the ropin', at that, eh, Day? She didn't do so bad."

The Prosecutor's voice cut in insistently. "And in the face of all this evidence, Defendant offers nothing in the way of contradictory proof. Denial, yes." The speaker's tone was one of tolerance. "He says, 'On the night of July third, when Belle Turner was murdered, I was asleep. I went to bed soon after dark.' Perhaps he did. But that he did not *stay* in bed, that much we know. He says, 'I never saw this girl.' He says, 'These people are mistaking me for someone else.'

"I must confess, I am surprised. Surprised that any man should risk his life upon so flimsy a defense. But then he must have thought that he was safe. He thought that he had covered up his tracks too well to need an alibi."

Day thought, "If *I* had been coverin' tracks that night, I never would've gossiped with that hotel clerk! Whoever did this was a fool!"

The speaker's voice ran glibly through his final plea. He made it brief and not too eloquent, and thereby imparted to the jury his own thought that there was little need for eloquence in this, a case already won by fact. He finished and sat down. There was a little stir in the courtroom; a rippling sigh through which the nasal monotone of the judge's charge to the jury was barely audible.

". . . innocent until proved guilty . . . burden of proof rests on the State . . . but if you find that the defendant, Lary Day, did murder the deceased . . . guilty . . . involves the penalty of death . . . reduce the penalty to life imprisonment . . . not guilty . . ."

Day shrugged and winced as pain ran through his shoulder where Lafe Turner's slug had struck. Pop Greer glanced up at him, his leathery face intent and anxious as he searched Day's face. But Lary grinned at him.

Blaine touched Day's arm. "There's a private room back here," he said. "It'll be cooler there. I wouldn't be surprised but what Ed Brown might rustle us some beer."

It seemed unreal to Day that in another room nearby twelve men were weighing a decision that involved his life. A deputy brought in a bucket and four mugs. Blaine tended bar.

"They just took a bucket o' suds into the jury room, too," the deputy said. "So you'll have time t' drink your drinks, anyway." He caught Blaine's frown and wished he hadn't said quite that. "But hell!" he thought. "Nobody but a fool would figure it'd take 'em long to get a verdict in a case like this."

The beer was cool, satisfying. Blaine wiped his lips. "Hell, Day," he said, "what made you kill that girl?"

Day met Blaine's eyes. "I didn't kill her,

Blaine," he said. "Why, shucks, I've told you that. I thought you knew."

"I did suspicion it," Blaine said.

Lary set his glass down carefully. "Knowin' that," he said, "I wish you were on the jury, Blaine."

"If I was on the jury, I'd vote you guilty in the first degree. I'd have to, from the evidence. Not bein' on the jury, I'm sort o' free to use what little brains God let me have."

"And so?" Day prompted gently as Blaine paused.

"And so I start to addin' up what I know about you. It ain't much, maybe. But still I've called a man's bluff in a poker game on less."

"Such as?"

"I saw you ride. I saw you come up grinnin' after losin' the championship by a break that was no fault of yours. I watched the doc dig the slug out o' you. My jail ain't a de-luxe hotel. Five or six hot weeks in it have been known to make a man some peevish. Sort o' sours 'em. But you kept sweet."

Blaine shrugged. "What I'm gettin' at is this. I wouldn't say you was exactly gentle but still you don't stack up like a man that goes around pushin' little puppies in the creek and knockin' girls over the head with blunted instruments."

"Why, man!" Day said softly, "I'm close to tears with gratitude!"

Blaine grinned. "I'm quite an orator," he admitted. "Which reminds me of the Prosecutin' Attorney. That man ain't bright in his head or he never would've pointed out to the jury how flimsy a defense you had. Seems like if I was on that jury I might figure that a guilty man would've had a better one, unless he was a fool . . . And, speakin' of fools, that reminds me of you again."

"And I thought you liked me!" Day complained.

"Don't interrupt. When I arrested you there was four of us there in a bunch. Old Man Turner throws down on us and he don't announce his intentions none to speak of. My back is turned so I don't even see him. But you see him, and you see he's got a gun, and unless you're blind you see that he ain't there in a spirit o' friendly fun! Now, if you're guilty, you know he's after you. Best thing for you to do is to grab me lovingly around the neck and swing me between you and that gun. Instead o' that, you shove yourself between him and me! . . . What made you do that, Day?"

"What do you think made me do it, Blaine? You're tellin' this."

"If you killed Belle Turner and seen that old wolf wavin' a gun in your general direction and bellied up to him in hopes that you could talk him out o' killin' you, then you're a fool and I was right before you interrupted me a while ago! On the other hand, if you *didn't* kill the girl, and *didn't* know the old man, then you might've figured he was after *me* and you might've covered me just out of a natural dislike for seein' a man shot in the back. Which was it, Day?"

"I didn't know you then, Sheriff," Day said gently. "Not knowin' you, I did wrong. I thought, 'This sheriff has wronged that poor old man. But still,' I thought, 'it's all against the rules to shoot folks in the back—even sheriffs.' So I butted in." He sobered then. "That's on the level, Blaine. Of course, to swallow it, you've got to take my word that I didn't know who old man Turner was."

Sheriff Blaine set back slowly, his shrewd eyes still on Lary's face. "Acceptin' that," he said, "how do you explain the evidence? These people all identifyin' you?"

"I don't explain it, Blaine. I wish to hell I could!"

Pop Greer slammed his glass against the table top. "I'm tellin' you they're all mistakin' him for someone else! Same as that Starr Landerson girl done. You heard from her yet, Blaine?"

Blaine grunted and stood up, frowning as he hauled the contents of his pockets into view. "I didn't get in touch with her," he said. "I wired the sheriff of Coronado County instead. He's an oldtimer down there. I figured he'd know what she was drivin' at and I'd save worryin' her with it. Here's his reply."

He thrust a crumpled yellow sheet at Day. Day's first thought was, "He sure didn't limit himself to any ten words!" He read the message carefully.

MISS LANDERSON'S REFERENCE TO GARY MUST MEAN GARY ELLIOTT STOP ELLIOTT IS BIG CATTLEMAN THIS COUNTY STOP FOUND PICTURE LARY DAY ON RECENT RODEO PROGRAM STOP SLIGHT RESEMBLANCE BETWEEN DAY AND

ELLIOTT BUT NOT SUFFICIENT TO CAUSE CONFUSION OF IDENTITY STOP IMPOSSIBLE ANYWAY THAT ELLIOTT IS YOUR MAN AS I CAN PERSONALLY VOUCH FOR ELLIOTT'S WHEREABOUTS ON NIGHT IN QUESTION STOP MISS LANDERSON HAS NOT SEEN ELLIOTT FOR TEN YEARS STOP NO DOUBT IN MY MIND THAT ACCOUNTS FOR HER ERROR

                  LEMUEL MARSDEN
        SHERIFF, CORONADO COUNTY

Inanely, Lary thought, "Ten years, not eight. That makes her twenty-three years old."

He said, "He didn't aim to leave any doubt about it, did he? He took pains to make himself real clear."

Well, it had been a slim hope anyway. He dug thoughtfully into the pocket of his shirt, found a cigarette and lighted it. Deputy Ed Brown gathered up the mugs and the bucket in which he had brought the beer and left the room.

A court attendant thrust his head through the door and called to Blaine. Blaine glanced at Day, shrugged carelessly and stepped outside.

There was but one window in the room and one door. Outside the window was the street, now jammed with men. Blaine pulled the door shut after him. His voice, partly muffled by the wooden barrier, came back to Day.

Pop Greer leaned forward suddenly, his urgent hand on Lary's arm. "Doggone!" he whispered huskily. "I thought I'd never get a chance t' speak t' you! You listen, son! There ain't no doubtin' what the verdict's goin' to be. You sabe that. So Blaine'll have to take you to the pen. The capital's four hundred miles from here by rail. It's eighty by the wagon road. So Blaine'll take you in his car . . . You gettin' this?"

Day nodded wonderingly.

"All right. Soon as the verdict's in, I'm leavin' town. Got t' get back t' my pore beloved cows. This Blaine's an independent man. I figure he'll not feel he needs any help t' take you down to jail. You'll likely sit beside him in the car."

The door knob rattled but the door did not open. Blaine's voice lifted in some parting instruction to someone outside. Greer's whispered words raced on.

"If you're held up, you grab Blaine's gun!

Got that? You grab Blaine's gun! Hang on to it! He'll fight and he's a man I'd just as lief not have t' kill. You grab his gun!"

The door swung inward then and Blaine met Lary's startled gaze. "The jury's in," he said. "Come on."

Day crushed his cigarette against his boot and stood erect. His voice, low-pitched, was loaded with reproof.

"Why, Pop, you lawless, lyin' reprobate!" he said, "you never owned a cow!"

3

WESTWARD for thirty miles or so out of Sedalia, Blaine's battered, topless car fled noisily across a level land grey-green with zacaton and salt grass growth or china white where barren ground refused such covering. The last rain, long months ago, had slicked these naked spots into a paste which had dried beneath the sun and cracked into up-curling shards, like pottery. Sometimes, in the more broken spots, a curly turf of buffalo and mesquite grass lay like a russet carpet on the slopes. It was a land of faded coloring, subdued and lusterless; a thirsty land.

But now they left the plain and charged head-long against the foothill slopes that climbed by stair-step benches toward the blue escarpments of the Wigwam hills. Steep ridges and ravines came down precipitously to stem their charge and Blaine's little car growled stubbornly and spouted steam. Black tar brush made a tangled mat along the slopes and through it scarlet cactus flowers lay in vivid gashes like so many bloody wounds for which the yucca flowers, waxen white upon their lancelike stems, waved snowy bandages. Ahead, blue-black with cedar brake and pinon pine or mad with color where the sunlight struck on naked rock, the Wigwams towered tall and startled, saw-edged against the sky.

They stopped at Apache Tanks to cool the car and fill it with fresh water against the final climb through Parson's Gap. There was shade here and water trickled from the crevice in the rock to fall with tinkling sounds into a granite cup worn deep through countless centuries. Day waited while Blaine filled a bucket for the car then bent and scooped a double handful to his lips. The water had a sickish salty taste but it was cool. He stooped and thrust his hands into the cup wrist deep. The heat flowed out of him.

He said, "I hope these cuffs don't rust so we can't get 'em off."

The handcuffs were more Lary's fault than Blaine's for he had offered to dispense with them. "You promise not to make a break," Blaine had said, "and I'll leave 'em off."

But Day had shook his head, and Blaine had shrugged and snapped the handcuffs into place.

"I wouldn't want to be bound by any such promise myself if I was you," Blaine had agreed.

But now he chuckled as he held out a crumpled pack of cigarettes. Day took one and waited while Blaine struck a match. "We'd both be a damn sight more comfortable if you'd give me your promise and let me take them handcuffs off o' you," Blaine said.

Day grinned. "You worried, Blaine? Now, look. If you ain't enjoyin' this trip you just turn back. I wouldn't have you sufferin' on my account."

"Don't be so kind to me!" Blaine growled. "Next thing, I reckon, you'll be offerin' to tote my gun!"

He sat down lazily and squinted up at Day through curling smoke that veiled his eyes. "I ain't enjoyin' it, and that's a fact," he said slowly. "Each time I've made this trip before it's been with men I could despise or hate. I'm havin' trouble hatin' you the way I should; and I sure can't despise you much. It puzzles me. You stack up like a man, to me. Yet they proved in court that you're a skunk. It makes me wonder if I've lost my sense of smell!"

He grinned and flicked the ashes off his

cigarette. "Who are you, Day? Where have you been? What have you done? Before all this, I mean. Mind tellin' me about yourself?"

Day grinned. "Well, it's a long, sad story, Blaine. I was an orphan cheeild; no mother's love to guide me in my youth. I reckon that accounts for what I am today."

But mockery was just a pose, soon lost. Blaine watched the laughter leave Day's eyes and saw a sudden tightness draw the corners of his mouth. Day squatted on his heels and made a quick, impatient pattern with his finger in the dust. His hat brim dropped to shield his eyes.

"Pryin' into a man's past ain't real good manners, Blaine," he said gruffly. "I'm some surprised at you."

"A man can always refuse to tell what he's ashamed of, kid," Blaine said gently. "I can look at a horse and come fairly close to tellin' how he's bred and how he's been handled. I figure it's the same with men. I didn't think you'd have much to hide."

"Nor much to tell," Day said. "Till I was eight, all I remember is the San Joaquin Orphans' Home. It was a kindly place but it had walls; high stone ones with barbed wire on top. I wanted out . . . Pop Greer adopted me.

I don't know why. Maybe because he was lonely, too. He is a desert man, or was. Sometimes I went with him, prospectin'. But mostly I worked cattle. I liked that better than prospectin'. Ridin' came natural to me. I topped off some rough ones here and there and got to followin' the rodeo circuit. Pop struck a fair sized pocket about that time, enough to see him through the years that he's got left. So he took to travelin' with me. He's folks, Pop is. He'll do to ride the river with."

He broke off there and glanced a little sheepishly at Blaine. "So there it is," he said.

"Not all of it," Blaine said. "Greer's done a middlin' job with you, that's plain. A man can teach a broad-broom to stand hitched, you give him time. But it takes a good horse to carry weight and keep his ears pricked up . . . What came before San Joaquin, Day? You know?"

"Not all of it. When Greer adopted me the Padres gave him a letter. Pop gave it to me on my twenty-first birthday. It was . . . from my mother."

His eyes were bleak and empty now, avoiding Blaine's. This was a vault of memory kept resolutely locked these past six weeks, but now Blaine's gentle probing had dissolved the barriers. The wistful sweetness of that message from the dead came back to him.

It seems so strange to be writing this to you, a strong, grown man whom I have never seen because as I write it I can see you here beside me, so pink and small, so dear to me; my son.

But there are things that I must tell you, boy, and this is the only way to do it. Because I am dying, Lary. Please don't feel sad for me. Except for you, there's nothing I would care to live for now. But I wouldn't run away and leave you, dear, because of that. I have no choice.

I'm giving you my fathers name, Lary. Lary Daniel Day. But that is not because we are dishonored by your birth, at all. It is only because I have taken a step from which there is no going back and that step passes on to you an injury which should have been just mine. I don't want that injury to teach you hatred, son. That's why I won't give you your father's name.

If ever it is necessary that you know that name, you can find the record of our marriage in San Francisco. My name will be enough of a clue for that. But, Lary, don't unless you must.

You see, I loved your father desperately. He was so strong and fine, so handsome, he seemed entirely wonderful to me. To others, too. It wasn't in him to be faithful, you see. I should have known, and loved him less, perhaps. But when I found that my own sister, visiting us, was bearing him a child . . .

I couldn't face it any more, you see. For I was bearing you, then, too. I ran away.

And there was more, of course; much more. It was a long, long letter full of all the yearning love and hope that mothers have for sons; a letter picturing unconsciously the writer's own sweet gallantry and gentleness. And Lary must have passed that picture on to Blaine, for Blaine, too, felt the self-same tightness in his throat that Day's low voice betrayed.

"Her name was Lorna Winslow Day. I've never tried to find out more than that. I never will."

The silence following Day's pause was hard to bear. Blaine's voice was husky when he spoke at last. "She was a thoroughbred," he said.

"Thanks, son, for tellin' me . . . We'd better go."

He stood up and climbed stiffly back into the car. Day followed him. The engine started with a crackling fusillade of backfire shots, then steadied as it lurched ahead. Day thought, "I wonder why I told him that? I'm just a prisoner to him; a prisoner he can't hate and wonders why."

Steep walls sprang up on either side of them and presently they climbed through welcome shade along a trail that pitched up steeply through a turmoil of up-thrusting rock. The canyon narrowed gradually and for a time they crept between sheer walls within an arm's length on either side; and here the engine's roar became a thunderous flood of sound that cut them off, marooned them in a world in which there was no other sense but that of sound.

It was a gloomy place, filled with a chill foreboding and a patient threat. A place Day thought, for ambush. He glanced at Blaine and knew that he, too, felt danger here. Blaine had reversed his belt so that his gun lay snug between his left hip and the body of the car, butt forward, easily accessible to him but not to Day. But now his brown hands on the wheel were tense and he sat stiff against the lurching of the car, his eyes alert and restless on the road ahead.

Once when a heavier jolt flung Day against his arm, Blaine thrust him back with startled force and Lary laughed. Blaine's glance combined apology and gloomy reproach. The motor's roar died to a whisper as the grade decreased and Blaine's voice came through it, edged and sharp.

"Damn spooky place! I got to wonderin', just now, why Greer pulled out so suddenlike. And that reminded me what a simple matter it'd be for a man to rise up on one o' them ledges after we passed and put a slug between my shoulder blades! It sort o' made me wish I'd taken you around by train."

Yet, when it happened, it was not a startling thing.

They had crossed the backbone of the ridge so that the car ran lightly on the further slope. The deafening, nerve-wracking roar was gone. Here, too, the walls stood wide apart so that the sun struck slantingly into the depths. Blaine settled back, at ease again. Not even when he saw the rock that blocked the trail beyond a sharp, brush-hidden curve did he identify it as the thing that he had feared.

He stopped the car and growled an oath. "These doggone cliffs are always sheddin' rock," he said. "We'll have to roll that thing aside. There's no way past."

But Lary knew. The voice that came out of the thicket back of them was no surprise to him.

"Set steady, Blaine. It's all in fun. Put up your hands."

Blaine's left hand on the latch released the door as Pop's first words rang out. He stiffened, swung his legs out past the running board and slid. An instant more and he would have twisted out beneath the steering wheel and down into the shelter of the car. It was a crafty movement, worthy of success. But Day's swift lunge defeated it. His two hands closed on Blaine's right arm. Blaine's weight jerked him against the steerlng wheel. Between the spokes, he met Blaine's angry eyes and grinned.

"You crazy fool!" Day said admiringly. "At that, you like to've got away with it! . . . Hold steady now till Pop collects your gun."

From somewhere back of them Pop Greer called anxiously, "You got him, son?"

"It's okay, Pop," Day said. "Come get his gun."

Greer came out from behind the car, a rifle held in front of him, waist high. But he grinned as he took in the scene. "By jacks!" he said. "He like t' fooled us, didn't he?" He stepped back warily, possessed of Blaine's gun. "Now turn him loose. It's lucky that I ain't a nervous man. By gollies, seein' you drop out of sight like that, I might've poked a bullet through the back o' that seat. You ought t' thank me, Blaine! Not gettin' startled like I might've done, I saved your life!"

Blaine twisted and stood erect. "You sawed-off runt!" he said but there was little rancor in his voice. "You would've shot, all right, only you was scared o' hittin' Day instead o' me! *You saved my life!*"

He snorted as the weight of that remark came home to him. "Why, you—!" Words failed him, but his look was eloquent.

Pop grinned. "Why, Sheriff, that's unkind of you! Belittlin' my motives that-a-way! I'm grieved. You search him, son. He's got a nasty mind, that man. He's apt t' have a gun hid out on us."

But Lary's search revealed no hidden gun.

Nor did it yield the key to the handcuffs. He mentioned that. Blaine grinned at him.

"Why, shucks!" Blaine murmured, very mild. "I must've plumb misplaced that key! Now, that's too bad! I hate to inconvenience you this way."

Greer scowled at him. "There, there!" he soothed. "We'll get along all right. I brought a hacksaw, just in case. You get it, son. You'll find a pair o' horses hid behind the thicket there. Go lead 'em out. The hacksaw's in the saddle pocket on the black."

The horses were well hidden in a pocket close against the canyon wall; Pop Greer's own black and a dun-colored horse that Day had never seen before. He led them out beside the car. There was a hacksaw in the saddle pocket!

"By God!" said Blaine. "That's what I call preparedness!" He shrugged, surrendering. "The key's inside the sweatband in my hat, doggone your hides! No use your sawin' up a brand-new pair of cuffs."

He sat down calmly on the fender of the car and watched Pop Greer unlock the cuffs. "You know," he said, "I almost hope you get away with it! Almost; not quite. I hate to lose a prisoner . . . At that, I ain't exactly losin' you.

I sort o' looked for this; took steps accordingly. You won't get far . . . It's too bad, too, when you stop to think of it."

He lit a cigarette and grinned. "Day, now, ain't riskin' much, not havin' anything t' lose, so t' speak. But Greer! My, my! The charges I'll be forced to bring against that man! Assault with a deadly weapon; that's just one of 'em. Interferin' with an officer in the performance o' his duty; that's another one. Aidin' and abettin' the escape of a prisoner; that's three . . . Tut, tut! The poor old man! He'll die in jail, most like."

Greer said, "You think we ought t' shoot him, son? Just t' put him out o' his misery, I mean? Poor devil, grievin' that-a-way; it's downright sad!"

Day's answer came from underneath the car's uplifted hood. "Oh, let him live," he said generously. "And suffer!"

He straightened, grinning as he met Blaine's gaze. "I've taken the innards out of the timer, Blaine," he said. "It won't cost you much to make repairs, once you get to where they sell 'em. But the car won't run."

Day's wordly goods were in the tonneau of Blaine's car and from them now he sorted out his spurs, slicker and a pair of well-filled saddle bags. He took Blaine's gun from Greer and thrust it down inside the waistband of his pants. Greer strapped the saddle bags behind the saddle on the dun and mounted while Day buttoned on his spurs. He straightened then and glanced at Blaine.

"I sort of hate to do this to you, Blaine," he said, quite honestly. "You've been damn good to me."

Blaine let that pass. "That gun—" He paused and grinned a little crookedly. "I'll be trailin' you, you know. Knowin' that you're heeled might make a difference, happen we should meet again. You—burnin' all the bridges, Day?"

Day nodded soberly. "Why not?" he said. And for the first time Blaine was conscious of his bitterness. "I'd sooner take a bullet than a rope, I reckon. The tail goes with the hide. You come a-shootin', Blaine. Or send some other man. The last, by preference. I'd hate to have to shoot at you."

He mounted and the dun horse carried him around the rock that blocked the trail. Greer followed him and Blaine stood up to watch them go. "So long!" Day's voice ran back and Blaine called after them, "Good luck!"

"I mean it, too!" he said, beneath his breath. The thought somehow bewildered him. "I'd be damn glad if they got clear! . . . But, hell, they won't."

He glanced up at the sun and frowned. "It's after two. By three, they'll be expectin' us. By four, they'll begin to wonder. By dark, there'll be a net spread out for them. They can't get through . . . I almost wish I hadn't been so cussed smart!"

4

A MILE below the western mouth of Parson's Gap, Pop Greer and Lary Day turned southward on a dim, unlikely trail that paralleled the sawtooth summits of the Wigwam range. They took the turning at a walk and, for a dozen yards or so, Greer's black and Lary's dun moved side by side. Day leaned aside and laid his fist against Pop's jaw. The six-inch shove was a caress.

"Thanks, Pop."

"Aw, hell!" Pop growled deprecatingly. "Don't mention it!" Day laughed, not happily. "You needn't worry, Pop. From the looks of things, I'm hardly apt to tell a soul!"

He nodded, thoughtfully: "Blaine phoned before we left Sedalia, Pop. He told 'em we'd be there by three. By four or so they'll start men out to block the trails."

Greer chuckled. "You leave that to me!" he said, and forged ahead.

It was no wagon road, this trail, not yet a bridle path; and yet they made good time on it for mounted men in such a land. It was a trail laid out by a surveyor equal to the best: a cow. For even in its seeming aimlessness that trail marked out the easiest, if not the straightest, route between two points of interest to the cow; a route corrected and improved by later cows until in time the way was marked. It clung, at times, precariously to ledges overhanging heady depths and there were detours by the score past various barriers; but always, stubbornly, the trail held closely to the contour lines or crossed them only where the grade was easiest.

Greer's black horse set the pace at a swift running walk that broke occasionally into a trot. It was a pace that would put miles behind a man between sunrise and dark and leave him with a mount fit for another day. Wise men leave galloping to fools where distance is involved and Greer was wise.

Westward sixty miles or so, the gold-tipped summits of Sierra Verde cut out a jagged horizon. Between, beyond the foothill buttresses, a sea of emptiness spread flat from range to range; a misty sea cut here and there by islands where some higher mesa sought the sun. Somewhere beneath that sea, Day knew, was the Mal Pais, black, hot and terrible; a lava river vomited from some volcanic hell. There, certainly, was sanctuary of a kind, but Day had no desire for it.

And, hidden by that same thin veil, well to the north, were the state capital and the penitentiary to which Blaine would have taken him. Day thought of it as a grim maze of walls; stone walls like those he had once known, but higher, gloomier. He shivered as from cold.

A dozen times in that five-hour ride Day faltered on the verge of speech. What were Pop's plans? How did he hope to penetrate the cordon that must now be formed ahead of them and all around? Here was a land as large as England, possibly, with higher hills and deeper dells and countless hideaways; and yet it was, Day knew, a trap. The mountain barriers had but just so many gates. Those gates would all be closed to him. And, later, the encircling net would tighten gradually until . . .

But it was easier to . . . drift. The thrill of his escape died out of him and left a flat and tasteless emptiness. Now that the thing was done he wondered if it had been worth while. Escape—to what? The freedom of a fugitive was, at best, a sterile joy. And brief. The nervous strain of six long weeks washed back upon him in a wave of weariness. His mind felt limp. Somewhere to the north and south and east and west men rode to capture him. He knew that but he hardly cared. Inertia smothered him.

The sun was still visible above Sierra Verde when Greer drew rein at last upon a jutting shoulder overlooking Wigwam Gap. Behind them now was the last peak of the short Wigwam range and, to the south, the land dropped off in wooded slopes to where a creek, thinned to a trickle by the months of drought, turned sharply past the final hill. But beyond the stream was turmoil again, for there the land shot up precipitously to form the apex of the V-shaped junction of the Smokies with the Antelopes; a mighty, northward-pointing arrowhead a hundred miles on either wing, the Smokies reaching south and east, the Antelopes southwest until they almost grazed Sierra Verde.

Cool evening shadow lay upon the lowlands now; shade that spread and climbed along the slopes towards the peaks. And there were roads down there; great, grey-white serpents lying torpid from the long day's heat. A broad paved highway from the east pierced Wigwam Gap and then curved south and west along the foothills of the Antelopes. Two other roads, also paved but narrower, came down from either side of the Wigwams to join the first; one from Sedalia to the north and east, one from the capital to north and west.

And in the timber where these three roads met, Day caught the stir of movement and the gleam of fresh new lumber and white paint. A car shot into view far to the east, a bug swift-moving on a milky stream. It halted briefly at the junction of the roads, then shot away again. The motor's faint, far song came up to them belatedly.

"Light, son," Greer said, "and let your saddle rest. We'd better not go down till dark. Here's where we talk."

Day swung down, a little stiff and saddle-sore. Six weeks in jail had softened him a little. The next few days would harden him, he guessed; hard days and nights of riding, weary and unfed, pursued, nerves wearing raw, with fear for company. "Or maybe it won't last that long," he thought. "It may end soon."

The clipped, staccato sound of hammering came up to them, intermittent and subdued. Day found a cigarette; lit it; stretched, and nodded down the slope. "Somebody's buildin' him a house," he said. "A fillin' station, probably, and a hot-dog stand. We'll have to circle that."

But Greer said, "No. That's where we're headed for."

Day turned to stare at him.

"What's more," Greer said, "it ain't a hot-dog stand. A fillin' station, yes; and a damn good place for one, too, if you're askin' me. Meals, maybe, later on. But those are sidelines. That, my son, is Danny Lightfoot's Indian Store; official outlet for Reservation products; blankets, rugs, bead work, et cetera. Et cetera meanin' candy bars and soda pop."

Day's grin was slow, incredulous. "The hell!" he said. "So Danny's cashin' in his chips and settlin' down! He's smart, at that. A man keeps forkin' 'em long enough, they'll smash him up. I'll miss that Indian, though. He's one top hand."

He broke off suddenly and shot a guilty glance at Greer. "I forgot . . . The *crowds'll* miss him. I won't be there."

He looked away and Greer kept silent for a little while. It was no easy thing, Greer knew, to see the framework of your life smashed down from under you; a structure you have built up piece by piece wrecked hopelessly beyond repair. As well, he thought, to let the boy get used to it. "Because my plans may fail," Greer thought. "I'm gamblin' in the dark."

His voice was gentle when he spoke at last. "Danny ain't exactly quittin', though. You see, he's married, Danny is. Right after the Sedalia show he married him a squaw. Damn pretty kid; smart, too. She's been to school. This thing is her idea, in fact. Them Reservation Indians turn out a lot o' stuff in a year, and like as not get gypped out of it. She figures she can take some of it and pay a fair price for it and still make a profit sellin' it to tourists and the like. So Danny's usin' his Sedalia winnin's to set her up in business. Soon as she's established, he aims to hit the rodeos again and cash in on his championship."

He glanced at Day; saw the tautness leave the lines around Day's mouth and jaw.

"It was right lucky, the way I stumbled onto Danny. As soon as I heard the verdict, I hauled out. That was a week ago. O' course, they got to wait a year before they hang a man in this state, but I figured it'd be a damn sight easier to get you loose before they landed you in any big-town jail. So I took a look at the lay o' the land, figurin' all the time that Blaine'd take you in his car. Well, I found this trail we rode today and followed it down to the road yonder. And there was Danny."

So far, Day's interest was casual, impersonal. Yet he was conscious of a growing tension in Greer's voice. He wondered why.

"Danny introduced me to his wife and told me what he was aimin' to do. Then, casual-like, he says, 'I'm glad to know that Day got clear. I seen him the other day, down in Coronado, but I didn't get to speak to him. He sure had that Sedalia show sewed up and in the bag until that black horse took that crazy dive. That boy can ride!'"

Day straightened suddenly. "Coronado?"

Greer nodded eagerly. "You get it, too, eh? Well, son, it like to knocked me for a loop! O' course, I sort o' smelled a rat when Blaine showed us that telegram. Seemed queer t' me that a man should use up all them words. The only telegrams I ever got was short and sweet! But then I got t' figurin' and it occurred t' me that this Marsden feller, him bein' sheriff and all, he likely charged the message up t' the taxpayers and didn't care how much it cost. That put me off the track again.

"Well, anyway, I says t' Danny, 'Hell!' I says. 'Don't you ever read the papers?' And Danny says, 'Not often, no. They're mostly all a pack o' lies, anyway. Why?' So then I tells him that they've sentenced you to hang and that you been in that Sedalia jail till now and if he seen you anywhere but there he must've seen your ghost. . . . And Danny says, 'Well, then, I seen his ghost all right; or else his twin. We'd just got through gettin' married and was on our way up here and I took a side trip over to Coronado to buy me a bottle of hooch from a man I know there, just in case o' snake-bite. And there was Day, settin' in a big car and talkin' to some girl.'

"Danny says he would've spoke to you then only just then he sees the man that sells him his hooch and when he gets back after that you've gone."

Day would have spoken then, but Greer rushed on. "Now, wait! This yarn's been boilin' up in me all day and if I don't let it out o' me, I'll bust! . . . So I get to thinkin', and I figure as many times as Danny's rode against you he sure ought t' know the way you look, and if this jasper down in Coronado looks enough like you so's Danny's fooled, that Marsden man sure didn't overstate it none in callin' it a 'slight resemblance'!"

"But Marsden said—"

"Wait, now! Sure, Marsden said that he could vouch for this Gary Elliott's alibi the night o' July third. I thought o' that. But look! Suppose Marsden and this Gary Elliott are pals? He'd cover Elliott in that case, wouldn't he? And here's another angle. Maybe Mister Marsden's figurin' on a little gentlemanly blackmail! He said this Elliott was a big cattle man. He is; but that ain't all. Gary Elliott is the son of T. J. Elliott, the copper man. He's not only a big cattleman but—he's plumb rich! T. J. Elliott built the Broken Bar outfit into one o' the biggest spreads in the whole country but he made his real money out o' copper. He stumbled onto a solid hill of it. I've heard the story plenty times. . . . So blackmail might be a real payin' proposition, mightn't it? With Blaine's inquiry to tip him off, Marsden might've dug out a fact or two and got this Elliott hombre where the hair is short!

"Anyway, I figure if this Gary Elliott is mixed up in the Turner case he's apt to be real worried in his mind by now. O' course. if he is mixed up in it, he's been readin' the papers and he knows you're convicted and all that. But even so he's bound t' be nervous. Somethin's apt t' slip. . . . And so I got him on the telephone!"

"You—*what?*"

"I called him up! I says, 'Is this Gary Elliott?' And when he says, 'Yes. Who's that?' I say, 'This is—a friend.' I bear down on that word, makin' it sound mysteriouslike. I got a hunch he's worried all right, just by the sound of his voice. So I says, 'You been readin' in the papers about the Turner case up at Sedalia?' . . . And then I *know* he's worried! He says, 'Yes. . . . Yes, of course! . . . Who are you, anyway?' And I says, 'Never mind!' I says. 'You know the place where three roads meet in Wigwam Gap?' And when he says he does, I say, 'I'll meet you there. Come in your car, and don't waste time! What I know is dangerous and it's apt t' explode if it's kept waitin'! And don't tell anybody you're comin', either. Because if you do, this thing will explode before you ever get here!' . . . And then I hung up on him!"

Greer sat back, chuckling. Day stared at him. This thing was big! So big that it took time to fully grasp the meaning it involved.

If the Elliott man were really frightened by Greer's call it must mean that he had guilty knowledge of the case. Or maybe not. Lary remembered hearing someone say one time, "You can scare any man by simply sending him an anonymous message saying 'I know all! Beware!' We've all got something back in our lives that we don't want known." But Greer had specified the Turner case. That narrowed it.

Too, there was the matter of resemblance. If Danny Lightfoot had been fooled by it, it must be real indeed. Real enough, perhaps, to account for the mistaken identity at the trail!

"So what happened, Pop?" Lary's voice was urgent now.

"He came!" Greer said. "It's near two hundred miles, by road. He made it in four hours flat! That was last night. He's down there now. The Indian's guardin' him."

Day stood up suddenly. His face was drawn and hard. "Let's go!" he said.

He mounted and sent the dun horse down the slope. A car hummed down from the northwest, its headlights cometlike against the valley dark. It paused at Danny Lightfoot's store and then shot off to the southwest.

Greer said, "That might be a posse, huntin' us."

But Lary did not pause. It was black dark among the trees but as they came down near the level of the road Day caught the glare of lights in which red gasoline pumps stood out like statuettes.

They halted in the fringe of woods nearest the filling station and tied their mounts. Headlights bored toward them from the southwest and swerved suddenly to bathe the woods in silver as the car slowed to a halt beneath the station's lighted canopy. The headlights dimmed, flicked off. Day led the way through welcome darkness to the shelter of the station wall. They halted there, both men a little breathless now.

Danny Lightfoot, picturesque in moccasins and beaded buckskin pants and stripped to a thin undershirt above his waist, ran gasoline into the tank behind a long, low, open car. A girl, her hair a reddish flame beneath the lights, smiled back at him.

"Are you really an Indian?" Her voice was low, throaty, full of an implied caress. An oily voice, Day thought. He watched the sweet, smooth glide of Danny Lightfoot's shoulder muscles under copper skin as Danny bent to cap the tank again. The man moved like a jungle cat.

Danny grunted solemnly. "Sure! Me Indian. Sioux. Me heap big chief. . . . Need oil?"

"No oil."

The girl climbed back into the car while Danny got her change. But when he held the silver out to her she shook her head and ran slim fingers down his hard forearm.

"H'mmm! Strong!" Odd how a voice could hold such slurring, half-veiled, unspoken things. "You keep the change, big boy. . . . Next time, you smile for me! . . . I like strong men!"

The motor roared; was gone. A peal of laughter rang from Danny Lightfoot's store. A black haired girl in beaded doeskin dress walked out into the light, hands on her slender hips.

"Heap big chief catchum paleface scalp, eh? . . . The damn blond hussy! Next time, *I'll* wait on her!"

Danny Lightfoot's teeth flashed white. "Aw, nerts!" he said. "Can *I* help it if the dames fall for this hooey? Look! Sixty cents, clear graft! You buy yourself a rollin' pin. You'll never need it, though."

He slid an arm around the girl and stooped to lay his cheek against her hair. Day, watching them, thought strangely of the ash-blonde girl upon the palomino mare that day at the Sedalia rodeo. And, suddenly, he felt alone and desolate.

Danny Lightfoot spoke without turning his head. "Come on out, Greer. Day, come and meet my wife."

He turned to face them then, his left arm still around the girl. His eyes narrowed slightly as they fell on Day. But then his smile flashed out again. "Kit, this is Lary Day; a straight-up rider. Day, this is Kit, my wife."

The girl's dark eyes were round as she held out her hand to Day. She smiled uncertainly. "There's two of you!" she said.

Greer chuckled. "How's the prisoner?"

"Asleep." Lightfoot lit a cigaret, his eyes on Greer above the flame of the match. "Carload o' deputies from up northwest just passed by here lookin' for you two. They drove on west."

"We seen 'em," Greer said evenly.

Kit Lightfoot's eyes were still on Day. "You mustn't mind the—war-paint," she said softly. "It's part of our show. The tourists fall for it. . . . Won't you come in?"

Day said, "It's fine of you to take this risk for me."

But Danny Lightfoot cuffed him almost angrily. "What risk?" he growled.

The place was bigger than it seemed from the outside. The big front room was public, faced with sliding windows open to the road. In it were piles of blankets, rugs, tables heaped with curios, a soft-drink bar. But back of that were other, private rooms. The place was gay with chintz and redolent of cedar and fresh paint.

Danny Lightfoot moved soundlessly to a door in the back wall of that bright room, and opened it. He turned to Day again. "He's still asleep," he murmured, very low. "Go in and take a look at him?"

Day nodded and stepped through the door. Greer followed him and Lightfoot lounged behind them in the open door.

This room was almost bare, unfinished yet. A window in the left-hand wall was curtained with a brilliant rug. Light fell unshaded from a small blue ceiling bulb. There was a packing box in the center of the floor and on it Lary saw a crumpled pack of cigarettes, an empty Coca Cola bottle and a pack of cards. A chair beside the packing box held a pair of whipcord riding breeches and a light blue polo shirt. On the floor beside the chair there was a pair of English riding boots with blunt, unroweled spurs upon their heels.

And, on a cot against the wall directly opposite the door, a man lay motionless in sleep, his face upturned.

5

DAY took a long, belated breath and felt his heartbeat hammering against his brain. He remembered dreaming once that he was dead and that his spirit paused to look back at the body it had left. This was like that. Unreal. Unpleasant, too, in some vague way.

He glanced at Greer, then looked back at the man upon the bed. The face there on the pillow was his own! It was like looking at himself in the mirror except that here the eyes in the reflected face were closed. There was the same slightly-too-large nose, the same cleft upper lip, so hard to shave, the same flat planes of cheek and jaw.

There were small differences. Day sought them out and fastened on them with a sort of stubborn possessiveness. The hair was brown and had the same slight tendency to curl; but it was darker. Just a little darker, possibly because this other man used oil to keep it down. Still, it was different. And there was a difference, too, about the mouth. Not quite so firm, perhaps; or was that just the slackness natural in sleep.

It was unnerving, somehow, to see the things a man considers altogether his the property of another man. Day felt, besides surprise, a small resentment.

"His mouth is different from mine." Day spoke in a whisper without knowing why. Perhaps he was not ready yet to meet those other eyes. His own astonishment was enough. The other man could wait for his!

Greer answered in a whisper, too. "Yeah. Seein' both of you a man can pick out differences. But still—"

Day nodded. "Still, they're mighty small, those differences. This might account—"

He paused. The sleeping man sighed heavily and turned his head. Greer stooped, caught up the riding boots and the clothing draped across the chair. Danny Lightfoot's hand shot out along the wall. A switch clicked sharply and the light went out. Greer's hand found Lary in the dark. His whisper rasped with sudden force.

"Take off your clothes! Get into these! There's a door to your right. It leads into another room where you can change. Go on! I'll follow you."

Day found the door and opened it. Greer pushed him through and closed the door. A light snapped on. This was a kitchen, spic and span, immaculate. Kit Lightfoot kept a pleasant house.

Day glanced down at the clothes he held, then up at Greer. "It's time I knew what this is all about," he said, half angrily. "Why steal his clothes?"

Greer shrugged impatiently. "They're lookin' for a man dressed like you're dressed; a saddle-hand, ridin' a mouse-colored horse. They ain't lookin' for a man wearin' peg-top pants and a glorified undershirt, drivin' a big yellow car. Put on them clothes!"

Day sat obediently; tugged at his boots. Greer's voice went on. "You see, I'm bettin' strong he killed the Turner girl. He *must've*, son! No other way to figure it that I can see; them witnesses and all. I aim to drag it out o' him. But, hell, I may be wrong! He may not talk. In that case, here's your getaway. His car is parked behind the house. In that, and in them clothes, you ought to get past them posses. They ain't apt t' know you by sight. All they'll have will be a description, mostly of your clothes and of your horse."

"That leaves *him* in a hole," Day said. "Suppose he's innocent?"

"Suppose he *ain't?* . . . But if he is, then he can clear himself."

"I'm innocent," Day said. "I couldn't clear myself."

Greer growled an oath. "Then we can clear him once we get outside. He must be guilty, though. How else—? And why'd he come, if he's so innocent?"

Day grinned. "What puzzles me is why he *stayed!* He wasn't tied. Doors, windows, car outside . . . What held him here?"

"He's scared! Scared stiff! I met him: told him I was just a go-between. Told him he'd have to wait and see my principal."

Day stood erect. The riding breeches fit to snug perfection on his legs. The boots fit, too. Felt like his own. The polo shirt was tight across his chest but not too tight. Greer ducked outside and came back presently with an expensive hat, flat-brimmed, low-crowned. The hat was small and Lary found a perverse satisfaction in the fact. It was another of those small differences that left him his identity. He valued them.

Greer took the hat again and ripped the sweatband out of it. It fitted now and Lary frowned. Greer chuckled happily. "That's all you needed, son," he said. "You're *him!* It's funny how a hat can change a man."

He caught up Lary's clothes and turned back through the door. "Come on!" he said. "Don't let him see your face."

The room they had just left was still unlighted now as they came back to it; unlighted except for the thin, tall shaft of light that struck across it from the door that opened to the big front room. Outside that shaft the details of the room were vague and meaningless. In it, the figure on the cot was pinned in sharp relief.

The eyes, wide open now, were blue. Day's eyes were blue; the same clear, liquid blue. But this man's eyes were troubled. There was fear behind them; fear that clouded them and caused that nervous twitching of the lids. Elliott reached up slowly and caught the lobe of his left ear between the thumb and finger of his left hand; tugged at it gently as he faced the light.

"Well?" The voice was harsh and rasping.

Yet it was like Day's voice in timbre and in tone. Hearing it Day felt again that sickish sense of unreality.

"Well? Get on with it? You sent for me; I came. I'm sick of all this damn delay!"

Greer's answer, coming from the darkness just outside the shaft of light, had a purring quality that made it somehow ominous. "Why did you come?"

"Because, damn you, I'd rather face blackmail than have it hanging over me! My coming doesn't mean—"

Greer's voice cut in, sharp and insistent now. "Why did you kill that girl?"

If he had hoped to startle Elliott into a damaging remark, he failed. The man's hard laughter taunted him. "So that's the game! That's what I thought! Well, it won't work! Day killed that girl. No doubt of it. What's more, he stands convicted for it and he'll hang! Just because I happen to look like him—"

Was that a slip! Greer pounced on it. "How do you know you look like him?"

The man was startled but he blocked the thrust. "Lem Marsden told me that. Marsden, sheriff of the county where I live. He said he had a wire from that Sedalia sheriff—Blaine was the name, I think."

But he was wary now. Day sensed it; saw the tightening of the man's dry lips. It was like watching the expressions of his own emotions in a glass. He felt, almost, that he could read the mind behind that face. It seemed he should be able to do that. Or did it follow that their minds would be alike because their bodies were?

No, that could not be true, Day thought. Because, by all the laws of chance and reasoning, this Gary Elliott was a murderer. How else could all that testimony be explained? Lafe Turner, Mary Ware, the hotel clerk, had testified that Day had done this thing, said that, been here, been there. That they were wrong, Day knew. He also knew that they were honestly sincere. Here was a man whose looks might easily explain that paradox. That in itself was strange enough. But this was fact. Another explanation now would be incredible.

He saw Elliott's troubled glance probing at the darkness out beyond that shaft of light; knew that Elliott was made uneasy by his own position in the light. Day had read somewhere that the police made use of that same trick. It places a man at a peculiar mental disadvantage not to be able to see the faces of his questioners.

"Still," Lary thought, "if seein' me hit him as hard as seein' him hit me, it might work out the other way, this time!"

Greer's voice bored in again. "What are you scared of, then, if you're so all-fired innocent? What brought you here, two hundred miles, at night, just at the mention of Belle Turner's name? It don't make sense!"

Again, Elliott's left hand crept up to tug and stroke the lobe of his left ear. It was a nervous gesture, unrehearsed and natural. It seemed to steady him.

"That's not so strange. Here's a man convicted of murder. I happen to look like him. If I'm dragged into it, some people are sure to think, no matter what the evidence may be, that I'm the guilty one. Not a pleasant rumor, that, for a man in my position to have floating around! It's worth something to me to keep well out of it. This is blackmail; I know that. But, up to a certain point at least, I'm willing to pay it. Not too much, but—some."

It was too apt; too tersely put, like a speech rehearsed and shrewdly planned, Day thought. Yet it was reasonable enough. Day wondered if his own quite natural prejudice were causing him to pick imaginary flaws in Elliott's defense. An innocent man might reason, he supposed, as Elliott had done. So might a guilty one.

Greer growled out an oath. "You got the answers mighty pat!" he said. "Bear this in mind; one of us here's an Indian. I've heard it told that Redskins know some ways o' pryin' secrets out o' folks; unpleasant ways!"

That was an error, Lary thought. Greer's power lay, if anywhere, in what Elliott might think Greer knew. This evident desire to make the prisoner talk was weakening their case, Day thought. Would weaken it, at least, if Elliott discerned the flaw in it.

Greer paused to let his threat sink in, then tossed Day's clothes toward the cot. "Get dressed!" he snapped. And then, in answer to Elliott's protest that the clothes were not his own, Greer growled, "Stay nekkid, then! We're leavin' here, that's all. If it was me, I'd feel more comfortable in pants. You take your choice."

Elliott cursed beneath his breath but he put on the clothes. Out in the dark somewhere, a horse nickered shrilly and the sound brought sudden tension in the room. Lightfoot wheeled instantly and stepped outside. Greer's whisper came to Lary through the darkness, barely audible.

"You'd better go! His car's out back. The key is in the left-hand pocket of his pants. I felt it there a while ago. There's money in the billfold on your hip. The car's full-up, gas, water, oil. The Indian seen to that. Make time but don't get pinched for speedin', kid. They'd have you then. Write Danny, when you're in the clear. He'll get in touch with me."

"Hell, Pop! You're comin' with me—"

"No, I ain't! Not me! Shucks, Lary, that'd spoil it all! The two of us together—? Why, the dumbest deputy would pick us out. This way you're safe. And Blaine ain't wantin' me so bad, I reckon. Not bad enough but what I can sneak through somewhere while he's huntin' you. That talk o' his was just a bluff. Good luck—"

"No, Pop, I can't do that! Leave you? I reckon not! Not after all you've done—"

"But, Lary, damn it all, that's just the point!" Greer's voice was pleading now. "All I've done is wasted if you're caught. And you'd be caught as sure as hell with me. As far as that's concerned, I'm safer, too, alone. Don't fight me, son! Go on!"

There was some truth in that, Day knew. Greer was a fox. He might get through alone. The net would hardly be as tight for him as it would be for Day.

He shrugged and turned toward the kitchen door. "Thanks, Pop," he said. "Take care of yourself! I'm headin' south. I'll meet you there."

He turned the latch and halted suddenly, one foot across the sill. Boots thudded heavily in the front room and Danny Lightfoot's voice called out a greeting, casual but just a shade too loud.

"Why, howdy, Blaine! What brings you here?"

Day thought, "Is that the Indian's idea of a joke?" Because it could not possibly be Blaine out here. Not possibly! Blaine, left afoot in Parson's Gap, could not be here!

But that was before he recognized Blaine's voice.

"Howdy, Champ," Blaine said. "Where's Day and Greer?" Danny's answering voice gave Day a mental picture of Danny's copper-colored face, expressionless, all Indian now. "What makes you think—?"

"Don't lie to me!" Blaine snapped. "I seen

their horses tied out there. I got your place surrounded, Danny. Bring 'em out!"

No answer came but Day heard Blaine's boots thud swiftly on the floor. A bulky shape blocked out the light from the front room and Lary stepped aside into the kitchen dark. And none too soon. Light followed him as Blaine snapped on the switch in Elliott's room.

"Howdy, Day." Blaine's voice was stilted, slightly strained. "And Greer! Well, well! . . . just take it easy, boys. I'm not alone."

Greer's voice, like Blaine's, was pitched a little high. "Doggone!" Greer said. "I didn't look for you, so soon. How did you manage it?"

Blaine's chuckle held a note of pride. "Guttin' that timer was a smart idea, all right. The only thing you overlooked was that the next ten miles or so was all down hill!"

Greer said, "Well, I'll be damned!"

"Exactly!" Blaine agreed. "I rolled the rock out of the way and coasted down. Less than an hour after you pulled out, I was borrowin' me a gun and a horse from old man Samuelson, twelve miles below the Gap. Did some phonin' there and then rode back and hit your trail. I'd seen, on my way down, where you turned off, so while I was phonin' I sent men in cars to meet me here . . . I reckon, Day, you better hoist your hands. I'd feel some better if I had that gun you borrowed off'n me. That goes for you, too, Pop. Reach high."

Day thought, "That makes three times he's mentioned havin' men outside. And there's been no cars drivin' up since we got here. 'Methinks he doth protest too much!' He's come alone!"

But still he waited, hardly knowing why.

Another voice came out to him; that voice so strangely like his own. "But I'm not Day!" The voice was desperate now, a little shrill, edged with a mounting fear. "I'm not mixed up in this! This is a plot! You can't—"

Blaine's curt command clipped Elliott's protest short. "Go easy, Day! Don't get yourself worked up. I'd hate to shoot you, but I will, you know. Put up your hands!"

There was a silence then in which a man might count to ten. The hinge-crack of the kitchen door gave Day a view of Elliott but not of Blaine. He saw a face convulsed with rage—or was it fear? A shocking face, unlike his own yet like it, too; the way his face might look, but never would, he hoped.

Elliott's breath came raspingly, half vocal as

he fought for words. He sank down suddenly upon the cot, braced upright by his outspread hands. Day thought his face changed subtly then, as if his fear were partially replaced by craftiness. The eyes were newly sly, furtive.

But Greer's words drove all other thoughts from Lary's mind. Greer said, with calculated treachery, "It's no use, Lary, boy. He's got us dead to rights, this time. It's too damn bad. We done the best we could . . . and lost."

And it was then that Elliott's eyes caught fire. He found voice then; a scorching flood of profane hate, all aimed at Greer. It startled Blaine. It was so unlike the man he thought he knew that for an instant his alertness laxed. He must have let his gun sag down, or possibly he glanced at Greer. Day did not know. His gaze was fixed on Elliott.

He saw the man's right hand shoot sideways to the pillow and whip out again. Light gleamed upon a short, flat, ugly gun. Flames licked across the room. Two sharp spat-spats, drowned by the heavy roar of Blaine's long-barreled forty-five.

Then silence, and the sight of Elliott's distorted face, wrung now by pain. His twisted body sagged, went limp. The gun slid from his grasp. Long seconds passed before Blaine spoke.

"God damn it, Greer, he forced my hand! I never aimed to kill the boy!"

"I know it, Blaine." Greer's voice was hoarse, as if from agony. "You couldn't help it. I ain't blamin' you. . . . He said he'd rather take a bullet than a rope. . . . He got his choice."

6

SHERIFF BLAINE turned the crank on the wall telephone in Danny Lightfoot's big front room and waited, fingers drumming on the boxed-in instrument. The receiver hummed sharply and Blaine's nervous fingers stilled.

"'Lo, Patterson? . . . Blaine. I've just killed Day. . . . At Lightfoot's store, in Wigwam Gap. . . . No, I'm alone. Send down a car. I'll wait. And, Patterson. Call in the men. Got that? . . . Okay."

He hung the earpiece on its hook and turned. Greer said, "I thought you had a posse here. So you was lyin', eh?" His voice was flat.

Blaine nodded. "Old Man Samuelson ain't got a telephone," he said.

To Lary Day, listening from behind the kitchen door, the following silence seemed unduly long. Blaine broke it finally, his weariness apparent in his voice.

"I never like," Blaine said, "to see a man get penalized for stickin' by his friends. Take

Danny, here; and Danny's wife. Just startin' up a likely business. Too bad to spoil it all by jailin' Danny for harborin' a fugitive. . . . And you, too, Greer. You're past your prime. A term in jail would finish you. . . . It's too damn bad."

"What are you drivin' at?" Greer said.

"Well, now. About the only reason I can figure for you and Lary stoppin' here is—food. Maybe Lary broke in through the back some way while you stood guard outside. Then I come bustin' in. Maybe you tried to warn Lary but I downed him 'fore he could get away. In that case, you'd be a fool to stick around, eh, Greer? . . . And it sure ain't Danny's fault if Day busts in to steal some grub. . . . I'm sort o' tuckered out, seems like. Mis' Lightfoot, you mind if I bunk down on that soft heap o' rugs till that car comes?"

"Why . . . no! Of course not, sir. Or—would you rather take our room? Danny—I—we stay up late."

"Shucks, ma'am," Blaine said, "I wouldn't think of it! Why, this is fine!" Day heard Blaine's grunt of satisfaction as he sank to rest. "You wake me when you hear that car. I'll catch a nap."

Greer cleared his throat. "You're sure a right man, Blaine," he said, a little huskily.

Blaine growled. "You still here, Pop? . . . Shut up and let me sleep!"

Day smiled into the dark. Yes, Blaine was right! This generosity would cost Blaine nothing, probably; yet most men would be quick to seek revenge for a defeat such as the one Pop Greer had given Blaine. Day guessed that Blaine would never sleep that night, despite his sham. The dead man in the other room— or, rather, the man Blaine thought was dead— would banish sleep for him.

Day started nervously as the door from the front room opened stealthily and closed again. Greer's whisper barely reached his ear.

"Lary?"

"Here."

"You heard?"

"I heard. Damn good of Blaine! Let's go outside where we can talk."

A slender moon hung high above the Antelopes and starlight made a silver tracery as it spilled through the trees behind the store. To Day, the night was beautiful. He felt, somehow, uplifted, purged; as if the dead man there in Danny Lightfoot's store had, by his dying, cleansed his living counterpart of guilt. This morning, every glimpse of life had brought to Day the threat of death, Yucca, stabbing up from tar brush on the foothall slopes, had but reminded him, "I won't see that again." The jagged pattern of the Wigwam peaks against the sky had been a threat of other walls, less picturesque, less spacious, soon to swallow him. But now the peaks, the moon, the starlight dancing on the leaves, the tang of the night air, held permanence. He savoured it like the aroma of a heady wine.

And yet he felt a certain guilty shame in his relief. A man had died—for him. Or in his stead. Or was that true?

Greer must have sensed his thoughts, so apt was his remark. "That man was guilty, son. Else why'd he take that risk? He could've proved he wasn't you. His fingerprints—"

"Blaine never fingerprinted me," Day said. "He said they'd tend to that when he checked me in up at the capitol."

"Still, Elliott didn't know that," Greer said insistently. "And there'd be other ways for him to clear himself. His hand-writin', for one thing. His not havin' the scar of Turner's bullet. . . . It would've taken time. of course.

That's why I pinned it on him like I did; to give you time to get away.... But he went crazy! He didn't dare to risk that contact with the law! And why? Because he knew, once they'd found out that there was two of you, they'd check up on you *both!* And, if they did, his goose was cooked!"

"Suppose you're right," Day said. "What next?"

"He took your place," Greer said. "Why not take his?"

Day gasped. The sheer audacity of that idea astounded him. "You're crazy, Pop! Why, that—I couldn't get away with that. And, if I could, why should I try?"

Greer's fingers closed upon his arm. "Look, son. I know you better than you know yourself. Already, you've begun to feel—responsible. And it'll grow on you. *I* did this thing, but you'll take the blame for it. You'll think, 'I sent a man to death to save my life.' And it'll ruin you! You've got to *know!* You've got to know that he deserved just what he got. You've got to prove that he's the guilty one, you see? And your best chance of doin' that is—bein' him! Find out who were his friends. Check up that alibi Lem Marsden hinted at. Dig back into his life! . . . You see?"

The idea took hold on Lary's mind. "But, hell!" he said. "I couldn't do it, Pop! You said yourself—that scar, for instance. They'll know he isn't me. And, anyway, I couldn't step into his life and get away with it! His friends— they'd speak to me—I wouldn't know their names. Same thing with his servants, and the ranch hands. Why, I don't even know where his ranch *is*, except that it's somewhere in Coronado County! Don't you see? It's crazy, Pop; impossible!"

"You might be right," Greer said, unwillingly. "I reckon, come to think of it, you are. Far as that durn scar's concerned, though, I doubt if they'll ever look for it. And if they do, his lackin' it won't trouble 'em. Blaine stuck three bullets into him and two went high. Where that scar ought to be, he's some tore up. . . . But the other thing—your makin' out like you was him—that's out. I see that now. O' course, his disappearance is bound t' raise a rumpus. Sooner or later, they're pretty apt t' dope it out. But by that time, you'll be long gone and safe. . . . And, as to findin' out who killed the Turner girl, *I'll* tackle that."

"How, Pop?"

"I'll go to Coronado. Shave off my mustache; folks won't know me then. And snoop. I'm good at snoopin', son. You write me there; Ike Brown, General Delivery, Coronado. No use our plannin' where we'll meet, because there's no knowin' where'll be the best place for you t' go. It's time that you was rollin' now."

He turned and led the way around the store. A long low roadster stood well hidden in the shadow of the trees and Pop Greer halted there. "There tis," he said. "Purty thing, ain't it? Ought t' travel some, judgin' by the looks of it. Danny said t' tell you it's a downhill grade out to the road and west for most a mile, so you can let her roll and start the engine after you get clear."

Day nodded and climbed in. The sleek, lank hood of the big car gave promise of untold resources of power and speed. Greer gripped his arm.

"Good luck!" Greer said. "You write t' me!"

"So long, Pop," Lary said, a little huskily. "Take care o' yourself!"

He reached down to release the brake and Blaine's gun, thrust inside his belt, prodded him. He hauled it out and handed it to Greer.

"Leave that where Blaine'll find it," he said. "That other gun—the one *he used*—I might've had that in my saddle bags. Tell Danny to suggest that idea to Blaine. He might get to wonderin'."

He slipped the clutch. The big car moved; gained speed. Day turned and saw Greer's slight, bent figure silhouetted there beneath the trees. He raised an arm, saw Greer's lift high in answering salute.

The tires struck concrete then and Lary turned the switch. When he released the clutch again, the motor caught with a deep, muffled roar. The car leaped forward like a thing with life. The headlights stabbed out suddenly to form a brilliant cone through which the road streamed endlessly. Day grinned and pushed the throttle down.

The roar of speed became a well that shut him in, alone and isolated. The sense of power thrilled him and he released it for a time, delighting in the whip of wind about his ears. But not for long. Headlights blinked up ahead of him and he reduced his speed. That might be one of Blaine's posses. Greer's warning, "Don't get pinched for speedin', kid. They'd have you, then!" came back to him.

It seemed a thing out of the distant past, that warning. Since then, a man had died. Day's mind picked up the happenings one by one. Greer's questioning of Elliott. Then Blaine's arrival on the scene, and Elliott's death. The turmoil afterward.

For there had been a time when it had seemed that Elliott might live. A time when Greer and Blaine hung over him and fought for that dim spark of life still visible. But they had failed. Life clung awhile inside the shattered shell, but consciousness was mercifully gone.

Then Blaine's phone call and this escape. The hands of the little clock on the dashboard of the car pointed to three o'clock. Six hours since Pop Greer and Day had stopped at Danny Lightfoot's store. It seemed too long—not long enough? Day hardly knew.

Another of Pop Greer's remarks came back to him. "He took your place. Why not take his?"

It was impossible, of course; preposterous. And yet . . . The idea fascinated Day. Gary Elliott *must* have killed Belle Turner. It *must* have been Elliott who had visited her in San Francisco; Elliott who had dazzled her with wealth, Elliott who had gone to her Sedalia room. How else could one explain the mass of evidence that had convicted Day? Those identifications by sincere witnesses?

Yet, lacking proof of that, Day faced a life of outlawry; a future haunted by the shadow of the noose and by the knowledge that he had forfeited a life to save his own.

And the proof must lie somewhere in Elliott's past life. Pop Greer would do his best to find that proof, of course; but Greer would lack the easy access to the facts that might confront the man who could step into Elliott's actual niche in life.

A dozen times Day thrust the tempting risk aside. "If I knew even a little of the background, the people, the manner of his life, it might be possible. But as it is—Why, every time I opened my mouth I'd hang myself. If I was dumb, I might get by. . . ."

"If I was dumb!" The thought congealed; took form. A man who could not, or who would not talk—"But I can't just claim I was struck dumb all of a sudden! It just ain't done! Some other way . . ."

What about this business one reads about in the papers? A judge back east who disappeared; people found wandering on the street, not knowing who they were? Loss of memory? . . . Amnesia! That was the name of it. Caused sometimes by a blow on the head. . . .

"Now, there's an idea!" Lary thought. "There's somethin' worth considerin'!"

The hands of the little clock on the instrument panel were perpendicular when Lary halted at a filling station where a side road curved toward the east around the southern outposts of the Antelopes. It was six o'clock in the morning of a new day and Danny Lightfoot's store in Wigwam Gap lay just three hours and some six score miles behind him to the north and east.

A man slouching sleepily against the nearest pump grinned at him as he cut the switch. "Up early, ain't yuh, Mr. Elliott? Or late, maybe. . . . Fill 'er up?"

Lary nodded and stepped out. His legs were cramped, but deep inside of him a warming glow of triumph fought the early morning chill. This man had called him Elliott! Without intention on his part, then, it seemed that he had taken the first step, successfully.

"Late," he said. The tantalizing fragrance of coffee and frying bacon came to him out of the neat white shack beyond the pumps. He yawned and kicked the left front tire. "Better check the tires, too, while you're at it. How's chances for breakfast?"

"Hot biskit, aigs, ham, bacon, flap jacks, and coffee fit t' float a monkey wrench, Mr. Elliott. 'Tain't fancy but it's fillin'. Step right in. Let Sarah fix yuh up."

It was not until his first breakfast had disappeared and left him still unsatisfied that Lary remembered that his last meal had been eaten in the Sedalia jail some twenty-four hours ago. The round-faced woman serving him beamed happily as she refilled his plate.

"Seems good t' see yuh eatin' hearty agin, Mr. Elliott. Last time yuh sampled my cookin' yuh sort o' pecked at it. Looked so worried like, too, yuh did. I says t' Henry, 'Mr. Elliott's either been sick or else he's gonna be.' But law, yuh look real healthy now, all right. Eat healthy, too. . . . They's plenty more them biskit in the pan."

Day said, "Why, surely I never failed to do justice to food like this. Now, when was this?"

"It ain't bad cookin', even if I do say it as shouldn't. It was the last time yuh was here; 'bout six weeks ago, it was. Maybe seven. And right about this time o' mornin', too. Yuh come down from the no'th, same as yuh done this time. Yuh remember? I says t' Henry, 'Any man that's been drivin' all night like Mr. Elliott, if he can't eat my baking powder biskit, he's sick, that's what he is!' Looked sort o' like jaundice t' me. Yuh know; sort o' yellowish and trembly-like."

Day chuckled. "Hangover, more likely, Sarah," he said. His voice was casual but excitement seethed in him. He drained his coffee cup and lit a cigarette, both actions carefully designed to shield his face. So Elliott had driven down from the north in the early morning of a night six—maybe seven weeks ago; an Elliott too shaken by some inward ill to relish food!

Why, this was easy! Ridiculously so, almost. Here was a clue, unsought, just thrust at him! It might mean nothing; might mean much. Of course there was that message from Sheriff Lemuel Marsden. Marsden had said that he could personally vouch for Elliott's whereabouts on the night in question. Still, Lary wished that he dared ask the date of his last breakfast here!

He stood up, smiling, and laid down a bill. There was a thick pad of them in the billfold he had produced from the hip pocket of the trousers he wore and his quick glance had shown him that not all of them were small. The thought flashed through his mind that that was luck. He would have cash enough to carry him for a time, at least. And checks might well have been an awkward snag on which to wreck his vaguely formulated plans.

For now he had a plan; a plan built largely out of hope but still a plan. That word amnesia had been the base of it. Thanks to the newspapers and the radio practically everybody in the world was now aware that a man with a head injury might, and sometimes did, forget a lot of inconvenient things. The names of his friends, for instance; knowledge of his old surroundings; even his own name. It was the sort of odd, outlandish thing that newspapers play up and that people talk about. Having read about it and talked about it, they would be quick to recognize it. It was not like some totally unheard-of thing which might breed doubt through ignorance.

On the other hand, it was a thing wrapped in a certain cloak of mystery. Lary himself knew little about it, actually; but the audience before which he played his part would know no more.

And a head injury was not a thing too difficult to acquire. An automobile accident, for example. Nor did the injury need, he thought, to be a very serious one.

A roadside arrow pointing east along the branching road just south of the filling station bore the words CORONADO—78 miles. Lary glanced at the speedometer. This accident of his, to produce the required results, should happen near enough to Coronado so that he would certainly be recognized. There was no sense, he thought, in having amnesia before an unappreciative audience!

He grinned and shot the car against the foothill slopes. Although the road curved south below the Antelopes it ran through country mountainous enough in any land but this gigantic one of towering peaks and it was well past eight when Lary topped the backbone of the diminished range and turned northeast along a narrow bench that ran for fifty miles or so toward the apex of the mountain arrowhead. And here he saw, for the first time, the vast triangle of the Coronado range.

It was a splendid land, he thought. Behind him, at the base of the triangle and beyond, the land was flat and scarcely beautiful. Northward, midway between the mountain ranges and some twenty miles below the apex of the triangle, he could see the flat white flanks of buildings where the town of Coronado snuggled cozily among the trees. A stream ran southward from the northern junction of the hills, roughly bisecting the triangle, and lesser streams ran down on either side to join it all along the northern half of its extent.

South of the town, scattered here and there, were other buildings, each with its curling wisp of smoke, each with its tiny checkerboard of squared-off fields. But, because he was instinctively a cattleman, Day saw it all as grazing land. Dry-farming, to his mind, was foolishness; a profitless, heart-breaking task. And so he turned his gaze again toward the north. For there, north of the town, there were no farms. There, certainly, was cattle range; a spacious land of rolling slopes and wooded breaks cut by the wavering lines of growth where streams ran down from either ridge.

All this before the underlying sickness of the land appeared to him. The drought was here, as everywhere. He had become so used to it that, even here, it had seemed natural; that dry, parched, feverish look; that barrenness.

The road pitched down at last in long

descending loops, and Lary settled to the task of threading steep-pitched, zig-zag curves. Ahead, a long descent broke sharply to the left and, at the bend, a steep dirt road thrust in at a sharp angle from the north. He grinned and eased his pressure on the brake. The car gained speed.

He glanced at the speedometer. Sixty miles since breakfast; eighteen still to Coronado. Outside the curve ahead, a wall of rock shot up a dozen feet or more, replete with jagged hooks and crevices. A bit too much speed on that curve and a man would have a perfect alibi for any type of injury!

The speedometer climbed to fifty. Lary slipped the catch on the door beside him. Fifty-five. That ought to do. Swing sharp into a skid; then jump. He had no yearning for the kiss of flying glass. Jump clear. The fall will be enough.

He swung the car into the turn. A black coupe jounced into view upon the steep side road. He groaned and settled back beneath the wheel. It fought him like a crazy thing. He found the brake. The black car shot ahead of him. He wrenched the wheel in one last turn and shut his eyes. The roadster took the outside wall head-on. He heard the scream of rending steel, the smash of glass. And through all that, another scream. . . .

He looked up vacantly into a pair of purple eyes. That must be wrong. Who ever heard of purple eyes? Well, blue eyes, then; dark blue and very worried eyes. Those eyes must be connected with the voice. Because the voice was worried, too. He focused his attention on the voice.

"*Gary!* . . . Oh, it was all my fault! I couldn't stop!"

He blinked and grinned. He knew her, now. It was the ash-blonde girl who had mistaken him for Elliott that day at the Sedalia rodeo. He knew her name, too. Starr Landerson. Yes, that was it. It fitted her.

Mistaken him for Elliott. . . . She was doing it again. Gary, she called him. He remembered, suddenly, the word "amnesia."

He closed his eyes.

7

THAT one clear flash of memory, then fog.

He was aware, vaguely, of cool soft hands upon his face, later, of arms around him and the girl's strained breathing close beside his ear. He knew that she was lifting him and he tried in vain to make his leaden body ease her task. Still later, he was conscious of the lusty roaring of a motor in low gear and of the motion of a car. But after that his mind went blank.

He came up gradually from sick, green depths. He was in bed. He felt quite limp and light, as if his body had no weight. He knew subconsciously, that if he moved there would be pain. He opened his eyes and saw a room of cool shadows cut by flat, hard bars of sunlight streaming through shuttered windows. Starr Landerson was bending over him.

She met his gaze. "Aren't you going to say, 'Where am I?' It's the conventional remark, I think."

Day said, "I'm different. This is heaven. I

didn't expect to go there, I'll admit. But you're an angel, and they don't have 'em in the other place."

"And you're an idiot!"

He let that go, watching the slow return of color to her face. It was a pertly oval face, softly tanned yet with a rich transparency that seemed to glow. There was no weakness in that face, Day thought and he remembered the strength of her firm arms about him as she lifted him. And suddenly he knew why he had made that turn into the Coronado road. He thought, "Why I've been lonely ever since she spoke to me that day!"

She leaned toward him and laid a cool, square hand upon his face. The movement brought her shoulder into light and Lary saw a smear of blood upon her shirt.

She caught his glance. "Your head is cut," she said. "I had to lift you and got blood on me. But it's just a scalp wound, I think. Chang telephoned the doctor as soon as he'd helped me get you into bed. It was your arm that worried me the most. It's cut quite deeply, I'm afraid."

He said, "I didn't know I had an arm."

"It's numb, of course. You see, I'm holding

it in a tourniquet. That's why I brought you here to the Broken Bar instead of taking you to town. I couldn't stop the bleeding properly and drive, and you were losing a lot of blood, and this was nearer."

He closed his eyes. Chang. The Broken Bar. The Broken Bar was Elliott's brand. But who was Chang? He frowned a little and spoke without opening his eyes.

"You know, I have a feeling that I've known you all my life. And yet . . . A lot of things are sort of—vague. I can't seem to recall—your—name . . . Or do I know it?"

He felt her startled movement but he dared not look at her.

"Why, I'm Starr Landerson!"

He tried to blend apology and vague bewilderment into his simple reply. "I'm sorry," he said. "I guess I'm still a little woozy, or somethin'. My head feels—funny . . . This Chang, for instance. Who is he? And the Broken Bar? And while you're tellin' me those things, would you mind just slippin' *my* name in somewhere? All of it, I mean. The Gary part sounds right familiar, but—the rest of it . . . ?"

He let his voice fade out, heard her quick intake of breath. She spoke in little gasps.

"You're Gary Elliott. And Chang's your Chinaboy. The Broken Bar's your ranch."

He caught the note of mounting panic in her voice and was ashamed. He said, "I'm all right, really. I just—"

He saw the look of listening in her eyes and paused. Then he, too, heard the rumble of a car. She said, with quick relief, "There comes the doctor now. Don't talk. It isn't good for you."

He had a glimpse of breezy bigness in a limp white shirt as the doctor came in and he heard Starr Landerson's tight voice say, "Here's Dr. Northup. Now you'll be all right."

Her gentle stressing of the doctor's name amused him secretly. But for some time after that he was not amused nor yet all right. There were bad moments when a needle stabbed red pain up through the arm that he had thought was dead and while blunt fingers, gentle but still torturing, probed his head. And, through it all, he wondered just how much this Dr. Northup knew about amnesia.

But later, when the tourniquet came off his arm, the deadness came to life in fiery agony that brought the black hood down once more around his consciousness.

He came alive again, filled with a deep and angry self-contempt. Fainting! Twice in the same day, too. But Northup's steady voice flowed into him and he looked up. All he could see was an expanse of Northup's back as he rolled down his sleeves. Northup's big voice had a soothing quality.

". . . weak as a cat now, because he's lost more blood than he can spare. That's all. He'll be all right."

"But, Doctor!" The girl's voice was low but urgent. "He didn't—know me! And he asked who Chang was, and what his own name was!"

Day saw the doctor's shoulders lift. "Not so funny, him not knowin' you, is it? You've grown from a spindle-legged kid into a damn fine-lookin' girl since that boy saw you last, if I remember right. As to the rest of it—He's got a touch of shock, naturally. But there's no sign of a concussion there. His head's as solid as a rock. Just like his dad's was! They've always been hard-headed devils, these Elliotts. You ought to know that, Starr."

"Yes, but—"

"Stop worryin'! Good god-a'mighty, Starr! You're nervous as a witch. A man'd think you was beholden to the young fool the way you act! He ain't worth it! And even if he was, he ain't hurt bad."

"I am beholden to him, Doctor. And I can't pay." The girl spoke quietly but it seemed to Day that the admission was a distasteful one to her.

"Don't be a fool!" Northup's growl was almost angry now. "I told Chang to phone Aggie Donahue. She'll be out here soon. I've got to run. Mrs. Jim Gillespie is expectin' twins and I'm likely late as it is. But Chang can take care o' him till Aggie comes. You find a bottle somewhere—ought t' be plenty of 'em around here, if they ain't all empty—and pour yourself a good stiff drink. Then you go home! Your stayin' here and makin' a nervous wreck of yourself ain't goin' to take one nickel off your debt to Elliott, nor off the interest, either. He'll collect the last red cent of it!"

She laughed, and Lary was surprised. There had been no hint of laughter in her tone a while ago, but now her laughter had a gallant ring. "I know he will, you old crosspatch! Even if it takes a deficiency judgment to do it! . . . But I'm to blame for this, you see. He might've made that turn all right if I hadn't skittered in ahead of him. And he took the rocks deliberately, Doc. If he hadn't—Well, I hate to think what that big battleshlp of his would have done to me and my poor little car! It was sort of—gallant!"

"Gallant? Pooh! He had no damn business drivin' that road at that speed!"

"I know. But I had no business driving without brakes, either. And I was! So you stop growling, now, and run along. I'm glad Aggie's coming because I'd probably be a rotten nurse; but I'm going to stay and help."

Day ventured a delighted grin. A vast contentment filled him and the world seemed good. The girl had turned now to follow Northup to the door and a bar of sunlight made a burnished helmet of her hair. It seemed alive and Lary wished, as he could not remember having wished for anything so trivial before, that he could run his fingers through that hair. But then he remembered who he was and what had brought him here, and all the joy spilled out of him leaving only consciousness of pain. When he looked up again that bar of sunlight struck upon a blank and ugly wall. Starr Landerson was gone.

That moment was a prophecy. The next ten days were just like that; moments of furtive happiness followed by swift plunges into gloom. Aggie Donahue took charge of him with a grim determination that was sometimes maddening. But she was kind, and Lary welcomed her because he would have preferred to die rather than accept from Starr the services that Aggie Donahue performed for him at first. She was fat and stolid, like a cow. Even her breath, as she bent over him, reminded him of fragrant, warm, sweet milk.

And there was Chang. Lary saw him only now and then; a stocky, ageless, round-faced little man with almond eyes, slip-shoeing through the house with trays or at mysterious household tasks. Almost a week had passed before he heard Chang's voice. When he did hear it, its clear, high timbre startled him. Whenever possible, Chang merely bowed and smiled.

Northup came at frequent intervals, first to dress Day's wounds, later just to sit and talk, his searching eyes intent on Lary's face. Day's seeming lack of memory puzzled him. Quite casually, in the midst of careless talk, he would insert a name, then pause and ask, "Do you remember him?" The same with bits of local history; a funeral, a dance, the time Ed Ackerly slept off a drunk under the church steps.

"Folks comin' down the steps shook dust down onto Ed and waked him up. He let out a yell and came out from under. Meetin' was just out and the yard was full o' folks. The look on Ed's face was pitiful t' see!" Then, swiftly: "But you was there. You sure remember that! You saw it, too."

The thing became a game. To Day, it was an amusing one. All the odds, it seemed, were on his side. To win, he merely had to look blank and shake his head. And as they talked, he filed away each name, each bit of fact, for future reference.

Northup, seemingly, was fooled. "It's a partial amnesia, I guess," he diagnosed. "That's one of these new-flangled things that I don't claim to know a lot about. Us country medicos do fairly well if we keep posted on the common ills. Long as I can do a fairly workmanlike job on a case o' childbirth, cure a bellyache and plug up gun-shot wounds, I'll be too damn busy to dig very deep into such things as this. Most o' my patients don't have this sort o' thing. Simple folks have simple ills, most times."

Northup's throaty chuckle was contagious;

likeable. "But I'm readin' up on it. What puzzles me is that you've got all the common, schoolbook memories—all the everyday facts like the days o' the week and so on—and all the mental equipment a man gets by experience, seemingly, and still you can't remember names or things pertainin' to your own past life. It ain't just a certain period of time that's dropped out o' your mind, as is the case in most amnesias I can find described; it's a certain kind of facts. Personal facts. I can't account for it. It's interestin'; damn interestin'. And time's the cure, as far as I can tell."

Once, Northup brought a man to Lary's room and stood aside. The man was burly, red of face and hair, with small, blue, furtive eyes. He was booted, spurred, in leather chaps and sweaty shirt; obviously a cattleman. And he wore a gun. Day's searching glance took in the low-hung, tied-down holster on the stranger's leg and catalogued it instantly. The man stood awkwardly, twisting a broad-rimmed, battered hat in ham-like hands as he shot nervous glances at the bed. And Northup watched.

Day grinned. This was a test, he knew. "It's no use, Doc," he said. "Who is this man?"

Northup shrugged. "This is Red Vale, Gary.

Your foreman. I thought you might remember him."

Day glanced at Vale again. "Well, Vale?"

Vale shifted nervously. "Doc thought I better sort of make a report, that's all. Nothin' new t' tell yuh, though. Cattle's lookin' bad, o' course. Range is burnt up. Water's scarce. But I reckon yuh knew all that. I've shoved the stock up close t' The Notch, but it ain't much use. All the cattle's driftin' up that way now anyway. They got the range about et clean."

Vale's voice embarrassed him. He paused, but neither Day nor Northup rescued him. He gulped; went on.

"Well . . . we're doin' the best we can. Hope yuh get t' feelin' better soon . . ."

"All right, Vale. Better go now." Northup's growl bespoke defeat and Lary shook with inward mirth. The test had failed.

When Vale had gone, Northup turned to scowl at Day. "Dead sure you don't remember him?"

"Dead sure," Day said. And then: "What am I doin' with a gunman for a foreman, Doc?"

"That's what some other folks would like t' know!" Northup snapped. He added then, suspiciously: "How'd you know he was a gunman if you don't remember him?"

"Easy! For one thing, he wears a gun. And he wears it down low, right level with his hand. No other answer, Doc."

Northup nodded. "No . . . And there's a sample of what puzzles me! You remember little out-o'-the-way things like how a gunman wears a gun, but you forget a man who's bossed your spread for more'n a year! It don't make sense!"

Day grinned. But the incident left him food for thought.

But it was Starr who filled those days for him. Sitting beside him, with slanting sunlight sifting through her hair as she read aloud to him, Starr Landerson wove magic into Lary's soul. This almost daily contact with a girl like Starr was new to him. So far, his life had been almost entirely masculine. Women had flattered him, amused him, sometimes satisfied him for a time; but they had had no permanence. Home life was strange to him and of a doubtful worth. In Starr, he found a basis for evaluating a mode of life that he had never known. A home with a woman in it; possessions; roots settled deep into familiar soil. These were things that he had overlooked. She made him think of them.

Not that she spoke of them. She was no flirt. In fact, he felt sometimes that she drew back from him. He knew, instinctively, that she disliked the man he was supposed to be. But sometimes, too, she seemed not to remember that. Sometimes her eyes were frank with friendliness only to veil, quite suddenly, with a bewildered doubt. He watched those changes, understanding as the girl herself did not, the cause of them. And, understanding them, he was immensely pleased. "She don't like Elliott," he thought, "but she's not sure but what she might like *me!*"

Sometimes he lost the music of her voice in the sheer joy of watching her. Once, when Aggie Donahue had left them for a while, he reached out quietly and took her hand. He had not meant to do it. It was an impulsive thing; the exploring instinct of a child to learn by touch. But it cut short the rhythm of her voice and she looked down at him, wide-eyed and questioning.

He said, "You're beautiful! . . . But then you know that, don't you, Starr? That I think so, I mean."

She did not answer him. She sat motionless for a moment, then drew her hands away; and

Lary saw her eyes go dark with anger as she looked at him. She stood quietly and put the book aside. Her visits were always strictly limited in time. "I run a cattle ranch," she had told him once. "I may not be very good at it, but at least I can be conscientious! And I'll be back again."

But this time Lary doubted that she would come back.

He spent a restless and unpleasant night. Next morning, ignoring Aggie Donahue's protests, he dressed himself. His wounds were nearly healed and further inactivity would weaken him. The doctor found him, when he came at noon, pacing the floor with restless energy. "I need exercise," he said.

Starr came again that afternoon. She seemed the same, yet Lary felt a subtle difference in her attitude. That difference, trivial but real, chafed on his nerves.

The following day he made a circuit of the house. It was a rambling, barnlike place, set on a jutting promontory. A hundred yards below the house the shelf dropped off abruptly and a steep trail plunged through tangled underbrush to a scattering huddle of unkempt corrals and barns. A rocky, rutted road curved south and east to join the Coronado pavement and Day guessed that that was the steep track down which Starr Landerson had come the day of his accident.

"Accident!" he thought. "I did it on purpose and got more than I bargained for, that's all. And I've been battening on her mistaken generosity ever since. Lettin' her think she was to blame! Tryin' to make myself believe she comes here because she likes me, when I know damn well she comes because she thinks it was her fault! Next thing, I'll be fallin' in love with her!"

It was on the tenth day following the wreck that Lary rode with Starr to Lookout Point. Three days of careful exercise had hardened him and they had bred in him, as well, a restlessness that would not be denied. At first, Starr had refused to go.

"You're not strong enough to ride yet," she had maintained. "And, anyway, I'm keeping away from the Star today—for a reason!"

But he had missed the gravity of those last words. "The Star's your brand, isn't it?" he said carelessly. "Well, if you won't take me I'll make Chang act as my guide. I'm through playin' invalid. I want to see this ranch of yours."

"*See* it?" She caught his words, repeating them with a swift passion that astonished him. "You've seen the Star a thousand times! Why this sudden urge today? . . . Or is it that you want to play the conquerer and watch the victim groveling at your feet? Well, I won't grovel, damn you! I may be licked, but I won't be humble! That's one satisfaction you will never have, Gary; never!"

Her voice broke oddly at the end and she flung away from him, leaving him a fleeting glimpse of stormy eyes brimful of rage and tears. He was amazed and instantly contrite.

"Why, Starr! I didn't mean—I don't know what you're drivin' at! I only wanted to see this ranch you've talked about so much—"

She whirled to face him. "To see! To see the Star!" She laughed, but it was not the clear, sweet laughter Larry had provoked deliberately and pleasured in these past ten days. "Why not ask me to show you your own back yard, Gary?"

He said, gently, "You're forgettin' my— infirmity, Starr, Even—my own back yard, as you say, seemed strange to me when I first saw it a few days ago."

His hesitant reminder steadied her, but even as the anger faded from her eyes they gained a fierce intensity that troubled Day. "Sometimes —I wonder!" she said, slowly. "It must be very, very convenient, Gary, to be able to forget —some things!"

It was the first real threat that he had had, so far, to face. The very ease of his successful masquerade had dropped his guard. This sudden challenge startled him. He reached up carefully and tugged the lobe of his left ear. It was his one defense; Gary Elliott's gesture; the one identifying thing that Day had gained in his brief contact with the man.

But even as he made the movement, he remembered that Starr Landerson had not seen Gary Elliott for years. So the gesture, probably, would be unknown to her.

She made a gesture of submission with her hands. "All right, I'll go. On second thought, I *want* to go! Tell Chang to saddle Blue for me."

But now it was the man who offered argument while Starr insisted stubbornly that they must go. And, in the end, Starr won.

8

THE ride back through the hills toward the ridge overlooking The Notch was a silent one. Day's silence was a product of a troubled mind. Starr's outburst at his mention of this trip bewildered him. A dozen times he would have questioned her but was dissuaded by the cold unfriendliness of her new attitude. Yet it was Starr who broke the silence finally. They had just crossed a dry creek bed and Starr halted on the further rim to wait for Day.

"It's strange," she said, "that creek bed being dry. That's Pinto Creek, you know, and it's always been the biggest tributary to Sweetwater south of The Notch. Yet it was the first one to go dry."

She glanced at him then and he saw in her eyes more than bleak unfriendliness. She was sorry, he thought, that she had spoken. She went on almost angrily. "I talk as if you were a stranger here!" she said.

"Suppose you just take it for granted that I

am a stranger," he said. "Everything I've seen or heard since that car struck the rock has been entirely strange to me."

That was the truth and yet it meant a lie. Starr glanced at him and nodded thoughtfully, but did not speak. And this time her silence troubled him in a new way. He wondered if she doubted him.

They dismounted at the foot of the last steep slope to Lookout Point and made the final climb on foot. Day halted once to glance with some curiosity into a caved-in pit that he identified from his experience with Greer. Someone had sunk a shaft in search of ore, he knew, and had abandoned it. "If Greer was here," he thought, "he'd find out why." He called to Starr, "Who owns this ridge?"

"I wouldn't know," she said curtly. "Nobody, probably. Why do you ask?"

"Somebody's been prospectin' here, that's all. I just wondered . . ."

"That's nothing," Starr said carelessly. "The hills are pocked with half-sunk shafts like that. Somebody found a nugget once, they say, in Sweetwater Creek. Since then, everybody who can't make a living otherwise has hunted for the 'mother lode'! Don't get *that* bug. There's no gold here."

They reached the summit of the ridge at last and climbed out on the jagged point above The Notch. From there, they faced the east across a narrow gorge three hundred feet or so in depth by twice as wide and possibly a mile in length. That was The Notch. To the right, the vast triangle of the Coronado range spread southward further than the eye could reach; first grazing land and then the town and, south of that, the scattered farms; a stricken land, charred brown by sun and drought. But, to the left—

Day caught his breath. A pear-shaped valley lay before him there, locked in by hills whose wooded slopes stretched back and up on either side to timberline. Between the slopes on the east and west, stretching northward from The Notch to where the mountains came together finally, was a vast acreage of meadow land. A creek ran down the length of it; the upper waters, Lary saw, of the same stream that tumbled through The Notch to split the lower Coronado range.

And, to the north, the signs of drought were barely visible. Day said, "It's beautiful!"

"Yes. Beautiful!" Starr's voice was low, a little choked. "Dad always said the Coronado range was a triangle with a pear balanced on the tip of it. You see? Star Valley is the pear. The Notch is the stem."

He did not speak and she glanced up at him. He was standing motionless, looking out across the valley like a man entranced, his eyes aflame. She thought, "It's as if he were discovering it!" And something in his attitude broke down the walls of her resentment toward him.

"So now you've seen the Star," she said. Without a conscious reason for it, she let her voice flow on. "Just above The Notch the land is rocky and barren, as you see. There's two miles like that, and in that two miles you climb almost two hundred feet. Beyond that, there's a hundred thousand acres, more or less, of deep rich soil with Sweetwater Creek running through the center of it. My house is at the upper end."

It was a relief to talk, she found. Talking took her mind away from the pervading ache that lay behind the words.

"It's strange that the land below The Notch should be so different. It's rich enough, but it has no bottom, seemingly. It's like a sponge.

Ten miles below The Notch, Sweetwater Creek is less than half the size it is up here. And, further south, it dwindles out. . . . Dad used to say that a dam should be built in The Notch so that the land below could be irrigated. He even had it surveyed. A dam a hundred feet high in The Notch would back up a resevoir covering more than two thousand acres, he said; enough to carry all the Coronado range through years of drought."

Day did not turn. He said again, "It's beautiful! Magnificent! The range below The Notch is good, but this—good Lord!"

His own enthusiasm startled him. He turned to find Starr's eyes upon him and he saw that they were startled, too, and questioning again.

"Your father felt like that," she said softly. "He coveted The Star. It haunted him. But you—! They told me that you hated the land. You must've changed!"

"Perhaps I have," he said. "If I ever saw that valley before and didn't feel as I do now, I've changed, that's sure!"

She said, a little angrily, "You own enough!" She flung her arm toward the south. "There's half a million acres down there—all the northern tip of the Coronado range—on which you own the water rights. Not all the land, of course; but it amounts to that . . . Oh, Marsden's Flying V cuts off a corner over to the southeast; and Gleason owns a slice still further south. But most of it is yours. Those are your cattle down there. Not half as many as there ought to be, in normal times, because you've let the Broken Bar go slack. But you could build it up again. You've got money. *You* could build that dam down yonder in The Notch and make a paradise out of that poor, scorched, thirsty range! Instead—"

Her voice broke raggedly. She turned away from him. Twice now this man had kindled angry fires in her that left her spent. She sat down on a ledge of rock. Her body, usually so straight and proud, was oddly limp.

He sat beside her; laid his hand upon her arm. "Instead?" he prompted, speaking very low.

"Look there!"

She pointed north and Day looked up. A rider topped the slope above The Notch and came down slowly toward the mouth of the canyon. Behind him, cattle boiled above the ridge and trickled down in a thin stream. The stream thickened, broke, began again;

became a sluggish river stirring up a dusty spray as it moved toward The Notch.

Day turned to Starr. "What does it mean?"

"It means I'm licked! It means I own the most completely worthless thing on God's footstool; a cattle ranch with no cattle on it! . . . And, three months from now, I won't own even that!"

He waited, watching her. She sat, leaned forward now, her elbows on her knees, her chin cupped in her palms.

"Dad loved that land. I love it, too. That valley's in our blood. My Granddad took out homestead patents on part of it; built a big log house where my house stands today. There wasn't any town down yonder then, not a soul between the Smokies and the Antelopes but Granddad and his bride. . . . Later, he bought the sections riparian to the creek.

"Those sections represent a lifetime of fighting debt. But Granddad won . . . And he passed on to Dad his passion for the land. Bit by bit, Dad bought. In the years before and during the war, money poured in on the wave of a beef market that fulfilled the cattlemen's old dreams. Dad poured it all back into land. He bought all that was left of the valley. That was his goal. But that meant debt again. Debt that would have been easy to pay off had prices held the way they were, but prices dropped. And dropped, and dropped!

"So Dad's life, too, was one long battle against debt; a constant whittling at a growing oak. But he made headway of a sort. When he died, a little more than a year ago, the debt had been cut to two hundred thousand dollars. Hardly a tithe of what the land is worth, but the mortgagor got panicky. He thought a woman couldn't run a cattle ranch!"

Starr's low, short laughter had a bitter ring. "I could have, though! But they forced me to cut my own throat! The only terms on which I could get a renewal of that mortgage were to make a cash reduction of fifty percent. I couldn't sell cattle to get that money because the market was terrible, and anyway, the cattle were my only hope. I had to mortgage my herds to get that hundred thousand; rob Peter to pay Paul! Even then I might've wiggled out somehow; but stock began to disappear. Rustling! There hadn't been any rustling on this range in years; not on any big scale, anyway. But now that I had desperate need for every head, they disappeared. I hadn't money to hire hands. There was only old Tom McElvey, and now and then some farmer boy . . . and me!"

She shrugged. "I don't even know how many head I lost. But it was too many! . . . that's what licked me, finally."

"But, good lord, Starr! That valley's worth a million, easily! The mortgagors must be a pack of fools if they can't see that their investment's sound! Why didn't you swing a new loan to cancel the first one. A bank—"

"I tried to do that, naturally. But banks aren't loaning money on grange property in times like these. And the present mortgagor's no fool! He knows he's got me in a jam, that's all. He wants the land."

Day sat in silence for a while. He said, at last, "How many head of cattle have you left?"

Her answer was delayed and he turned to look at her inquiringly. Her gaze was fixed upon him with a queer intensity . . . "Not one!" she said. "The man who holds the mortgage on the stock will probably levy a deficiency judgment against me, in fact. Because there aren't enough cattle left to satisfy his claim."

"Deficiency judgment." The words struck a chord of memory in Lary's mind. Dr. Northup's booming voice came back to him:

"Your stayin' here and makin' a nervous wreck of yourself ain't goin' to take one nickel off your debt to Elliott; nor off the interest, either. He'll collect the last red cent!" And Starr's voice, answering him: "I know he will! . . . Even if it takes a deficiency judgment to do it!"

That memory clarified still other things: Starr's passionate outburst a while ago; her attitude toward him all this while. He said, slowly, "The man who holds that mortgage on your stock is Gary Elliott . . . *me!*"

She nodded. "Those are your men, handling that herd. That's Red Vale, riding point."

He lunged erect, his face dark with a sudden rage. "By God, I'll put a stop to that!"

"It's no use, Gary." Starr stood beside him instantly, her hand upon his arm. "The thing is done. You've owned that herd for two weeks now. That was the object of my visit to The Broken Bar the day of your accident; to find out when you meant to move them. Later, I saw Brett Randall about it and he set Vale to rounding them up. That was four days ago; after Vale talked to you. He wanted to ask you about it, but Doctor Northup kept him out after that one time."

"Who's Randall?"

"A big-time gambler who speculates with his winnings, and your Number One man of business, Gary . . . Don't you honestly remember all this?"

"I certainly do not!" Day snapped. "Next thing, I reckon, you'll be tellin' me that I hold the mortgage on the land, too!" His anger startled her.

She laughed, a little nervously. "No. Randall holds that mortgage now. The loan was originally made by a San Francisco bank, but Randall bought it a few months after Dad died."

Day scowled. "Bought it, eh? If he's so dubious about grange security, why did he do that?"

"He wants The Star, that's all. That's not so strange!"

"Not strange at all! . . . You know," Day's sudden smile was whimsical, "I've got a hunch I'm goin' to dislike that Randall man!"

This time Starr's laughter had its old-time ring. "Oh, Gary, you're—funny!" She leaned toward him suddenly, her eyes more friendly now than they had been all day. "Can't you see how funny it is? I have so many reasons for—hating you, Gary. I *have* hated you. I've only tried to be nice to you these past ten days because I felt responsible. You must've felt that, even though you didn't remember *why* I felt like that. And yet, you've been so *nice* . . ."

She laughed at his quite evident embarrassment. "You've had me veering like a weathervane! I'd just get comfortably set on hating you, and then you'd—smile, or say something especially nice, and—I'd find myself liking you! You know, if you'd only got this bump in infancy, you might've been a nice young man!"

Day shrugged, uncomfortable beneath her raillery. "The more I hear about myself," he growled, "the more I am convinced that I should've been knocked on the head all right, a long, long time ago!"

The line of cattle reached down now into The Notch and Lary stood for a moment, looking down upon that stream of tossing heads. His eyes were thoughtful as he turned away at last and led the way back to their mounts. But it was not until he walked with Starr toward her car that evening at the Broken Bar that he brought up the subject that was in his mind.

"You said your Dad had some surveys made; about that dam, I mean." He glanced at her and looked away again. "You got the blueprints of those surveys, I wonder?"

"Why, yes. I found them in Dad's desk and saved them. Not that they're valuable; not to me at least. But they looked so—official, if you know what I mean! I couldn't throw them out. They're in the house somewhere . . . Why do you ask?"

He turned to her with sudden eagerness. "You don't remember, I suppose, whether those blueprints showed the line the water'd reach in case the dam was built? How far it would back up!" His own intensity embarrassed him. He shrugged. "You wouldn't know, of course—"

"It's on the maps," Starr said. She shot a quick, enquiring glance at him. "I remember Dad said it would back up about three quarters of the way up the slope north of The Notch and that the reservoir was really ready-made; that there were no low spots in that slope through which the water could run back into the upper valley."

She paused, but there was a question in her eyes and Lary cut in quickly before she put it into words. "You'll be back tomorrow, won't you? How about having supper with me? I'll have Chang fix up somethin' extra-special and we'll have a party. Celebrate my change of heart."

She shook her head, smilingly. "I can't, Gary. You're well now, you know. And I'll be busy."

"Please, Starr!" His voice was pleading but she shook her head again and put her foot upon the starter button. The motor's hum drowned out his plea.

He frowned, but when she turned to wave at him he smiled again and stood unmoving in the sun until the little car bounced out of sight around the shoulder of the hill.

He sat that night upon the broad verandah of the Broken Bar ranch house and watched the stars blink into life above the Coronado range. It was well past midnight when he crushed out a final cigarette among the little heap of butts beside him on the step and rose to go to bed. Hoofs rang sharply in the rocky yard below the house and he heard the throaty rasp of Red Vale's voice there in the dark. The words were indistinguishable, but Lary stood for a moment staring down toward the sound and weighing the potentialities in Vale's mysterious presence here.

The day of gunmen on the cattle range was past. A few oldtimers still remained, but their swift flight to fame was but a memory. Pop Greer was one of them. That fact had always seemed more than a little strange to Day for Pop Greer was primarily a gentle man. Yet Day had seen from time to time the careful courtesy with which the men who knew Pop's record dealt with him. Sometimes, too, in lonesome places, Day had seen the old man practice with the big, black-butted guns he kept in oiled cloths among his gear. There was a kind of magic in Greer's handling of those guns; a magic he had tried to teach to Lary with some small success. But it was an accomplishment, Day knew, that had no place in modern life. The roar of a high-powered car and the staccato chatter of machine gun fire had superseded the crisp beat of flying hoofs, the man-to-man and face-to-face shootout that formed the highlights of the bad old days. So why had Elliott hired Vale?

Perhaps it was a happen-so; a cowman hired to do a cowman's job, his past a mere coincidence. But somehow Lary doubted that. Northup's comment on the man had been a pointed one, not casual.

Day shrugged and let Red Vale slide easily out of his thoughts. But he lay awake for long hours after that, his mind too tightly keyed for sleep. It was a startling thing, he thought, how this new world had swallowed him. Ten days ago, he had been in turmoil, deeply absorbed in trouble of his own. Now, all that seemed far away. He stood, he knew, upon precarious ground; and yet his danger seemed impersonal, unreal. There was a ferment here that had engulfed him instantly; a seething whirlpool of cross purposes that he could not yet define. But he was part of it. He knew and willingly accepted that.

Just after nine o'clock the following morning he called Brett Randall on the telephone. His name brought suave and careful sentences of comment on his injury, of hope for his recovery. He said, "I hear that you foreclosed for me on the Landerson stock."

Randall's voice was self-complacent. "The mortgage fell due and I acted in your interest, Gary, naturally. And, by the way! I've found a buyer for those cows. Spot cash, and a small premium over the market price on account of their excellent condition. I'd recommend—"

"How much?" Day cut in. "The total, net to me?"

"Well, roughly, about ninety thousand, Gary. Possibly a little more; a thousand or so, depending on how heavy they weigh out."

"No sale!" Day snapped.

The gambler's voice came back to him ingratiatingly. "But that's really a very good price, Gary. Very good indeed. Of course, it's less than your—investment. But it's really very good. Naturally, you'll want to levy a deficiency judgment to cover the balance due you. There are, I think, some several hundred head of valuable saddle stock under the Star brand, and considerable chattel property; wagons, furniture, et cetera. . . ."

Day's voice smashed back at him. "No sale! And no damned deficiency judgment, either! You sabe that? . . . All right!"

He hung up. Ten minutes later he was calling Starr. Her voice, even across the humming wire, brought a familiar music to his ear. He said, a little gruffly, "Starr? I've got a proposition to make to you."

He heard her laugh. "Not over the telephone, Gary?"

"I'm serious! Listen! Take that survey map

we talked about and draw a line to mark the crest of that slope north of the Notch. We can have it properly surveyed later; but this will do for now . . . I'll give you five thousand dollars for a sixty-day option on all the land you own south of that line, said five thousand dollars to apply against a purchase price of one hundred and six thousand dollars . . . Is it a deal?"

He heard her gasp. A moment passed before she answered him. "Good heavens, Gary! *Yes!* . . . Or, rather, no! It isn't worth that much. You're simply being—kind. I won't take charity."

"Don't be a fool! It's worth that much to me, and more. In fact, I aim to make a skinflint profit out of it!" He grinned into the telephone. "What makes you think I'd be that kind to you, anyway? This is strictly business! Is it a deal, or not?"

"It's—a deal, Gary!" she said weakly. "But why?"

"I aim to build a dam!" he said. "Weren't you tellin' me yesterday that I ought to do that?"

"Of course! . . . But—why the odd amount, for one thing? That extra six thousand dollars—"

"You'll owe Randall interest, won't you? Six per cent on a hundred thousand for one year is six thousand . . . And another thing; I want to run my cattle on your range. I'll pay you the current grazing rental, in cows. This drought is goin' to force the beef market up and we'll both make a nice profit . . . But, I'm warnin' you, you better save enough out of your profit to share the cost of a fence between your land and mine!"

"A spite fence, Gary?"

"No! I'll cut a gate. But you'll have to pay for half of that fence and unless you come over here for supper like I asked you to, you'll have to pay for half of the gate! We ought to talk this matter over some; and, if you came, you might persuade me not to build the fence at all!"

He waited. It seemed a long, long time before she spoke. "I'll come," she said at last. "I can't afford to build that fence!"

9

JASON NORTHUP, MD. Pop Greer hauled off his hat and squinted at the trim glass sign with gilded lettering which hung against the weathered wall. The door to the left of the sign stood open. You walk into an office without knocking when the door is open, he thought. But at the door to a man's home you knock. This was an office in a private house. To knock or not to knock?

Greer took a chance. He stepped inside and rapped his knuckles on the panel of the open door.

A man behind a littered desk looked up at him. He was a big man, black browed and pleasantly ugly. The swivel chair creaked protestingly beneath his weight as he leaned back.

"Dr. Northup?" Greer said hesitantly.

"In person!" Northup boomed. "What can I do for you?"

But he was thinking, "Why'd he shave his mustache off?

He's worn one recently. His upper lip is pale."

Greer fumbled with his hat. "I want to know what's wrong with—Gary Elliott," he said. "Is he hurt bad?"

Northup chuckled. "Well, you're not alone!" he said. "This entire town, practically, is itchin' with the same desire! Most of 'em have urgent reasons for seein' him. You've got one, haven't you? You're his banker, or his lawyer, or his long-lost uncle, or somethin' like that?"

"Why, no," Greer said in some bewilderment. "Why, no, I'm just a friend o' his." But his voice was wistful and the doctor felt a sudden friendliness for him.

"Just tell him Pop was here," Greer said. "I would've gone out to see him, only folks said you wasn't lettin' him see anybody, so I just thought I'd ask . . . You tell him, will you? He'll remember me."

"That's just the trouble!" Northup said. "He won't! That's what I've been tellin' all of 'em; that he won't remember them. He's got a thing called amnesia. Means he can't remember things. Some things, at least."

Northup was talking to gain time. His mind was busy with another thing. But he could talk without thinking. He had had to do that so many times; reassure bewildered relatives while his tired brain fought out a battle-plan against disease.

"And these new-fangled ills," he said. "When I studied medicine, things were simpler. A bellyache was a bellyache; not appendicitis, or bad tonsils, or decayin' teeth. In those days, a head injury was a concussion or it wasn't. But now, good God! . . . I'll tell him, though. Just a friend, eh? Well, it's nice to meet an honest man!"

Greer turned but hesitated at the door. "He'll be all right, won't he, Doc? He ain't a-gonna —die, or anything?"

"He *is* all right," Northup said gruffly. "The boy's as healthy as a horse." He stood up suddenly and crossed the room to pat Greer's arm. "Don't worry, Pop," he said with brusque kindliness. "He just got a nasty bump on the head and a glass-cut or two. He's most as good as new right now."

Greer nodded and would have gone, but Northup halted him this time. "You'll be in town, I suppose? He may want to see you, after all. No tellin' what he may remember or what he won't."

"I'll be around," Greer said. "I'm stayin' at the Coronado House. The name's—Ike Brown."

He turned away and Northup stood in the open doorway, smiling thoughtfully as he watched Greer's thin figure moving down the street.

He was still smiling when he pulled a chair up close to Day's that afternoon to take the bandages from Lary's arm. A livid scar ran up diagonally across Day's wrist and Northup's blunted fingers moved with deft and gentle skill as he examined it. He spoke at last without looking up.

"Pop Greer's in town," he said quite casually.

He felt the muscles under his fingers tense spasmodically. The silence held while he replaced the bandages. He sat back then and met Day's gaze. "If all my patients were like you," he said, "I'd have to pad my bills. That arm is healed. The scalp wound's healed. There's nothin' wrong with you."

There was a little stress upon the last few words that lent an added meaning. "Nothing wrong."

Day's voice was low. "So—you know!" he said.

Northup's level gaze held firm. "Ten years ago," he said, "I set a compound fracture of the right forearm for Gary Elliott. I had forgotten that. I probably never would've thought of it if Greer hadn't set me thinkin' . . . Your arm has never been broken."

Lary nodded quietly. "I was a fool to ever think that I could get away with it," he said. "What do you aim to do?"

Northup laid his fingertips together carefully to form a wedge-shaped rest for his square chin. "I wouldn't say you were a fool," he said. "That arm—I'd be the only one to trip you up on that. And, anyway, you couldn't know about a thing like that. At that, I nearly missed it . . . What do I aim to do? I don't quite know. Suppose you talk. That might help me decide . . . What made you tackle it?"

Day shrugged. "You know, I reckon. If you recognized Pop Greer, you must know who I am. And why I'm here."

"He *said* his name was Brown. Ike Brown." Northup's smile lit up his erstwhile homely face. "But he wasn't sure you'd remember that. Maybe he'd heard folks say that you'd forgotten things. And so he said to tell you Pop was here. He was pretty sure that you'd remember *that*. . . . He's shaved off his mustache. That's what started me to wonderin', right from the first . . . I read the papers some. Pop Greer, I said. But I wasn't sure until I got my fingers on that arm of yours again."

Day said, "You read the papers, so you know the rest of it. That I'm Lary Day. That I was convicted three weeks ago and sentenced to be hung. For murder!! And still you ask me why I'm here!"

"I read, too," Northup said gently, "that Lary Day escaped enroute to jail and that he was killed by Sheriff Blaine in Wigwam Gap, resisting capture. . . . I don't believe all that I see in print, sometimes!"

"It was Elliott that was killed," Day said.

"I gathered that. And you're Lary Day, and you were drivin' Elliott's car when you had this wreck. . . . I've been through Wigwam Gap a time or two. Comin' down from there, a man has to turn off of a good broad highway onto one not near so good to get to where you wrecked that car. Seems to me if I was a murderer, drivin' a fast car, with an open road ahead o' me, I wouldn't make that turn. You did. I'm askin' why."

Lary leaned forward a little. "I didn't kill

that girl, Northup!" His voice was low but passionate. It seemed important to him now that he convince this man.

"All right," Northup said. "Go on from there."

"Meanin' that you believe me, or that you expected me to deny it?"

"Meanin' that I've got an open mind. Go on!"

"Those people identified me, Doc! Those witnesses. And they were tellin' the truth! They thought that they were right! . . . So, when Greer heard about this Elliott, and how he looked so much like me, we figured maybe it was Elliott that killed that girl—that all those people saw. But Blaine busted in on us before we could make Elliott talk. Elliott was jumpy and he pulled a gun. Blaine shot him, thinkin' he was me. . . . So I came here. I had to, see? Because if he was innocent, I was responsible, in a way, for *him*, even though I wasn't guilty of the other thing. It's all mixed up, but—do you see just what I'm drivin' at?"

"I think I do . . . But you could've gotten clean away, you know. So far, they haven't found out their mistake. They think you're dead. By comin' here, you put your head back in the noose!"

"I know," Day said impatiently. "But don't you see? I thought by comin' here I might clear up the mystery; might find some clue, some proof. The other way I would've been a fugitive."

Northup leaned forward a little. "You really think, then, that Gary Elliott was the guilty man?"

"He *must've* been! How else—?"

"All right, all right! We won't go further into that right now." Northup leaned back once more, his keen eyes right behind their lowered lids. "The way I see it, there could be just two reasons that could've brought you here. You had a clear track for a getaway, and you turned back. Why? Well, thinkin' Elliott killed the Turner girl and wantin' to prove that he did and thereby clear yourself—that's one reason."

Northup paused and chuckled. "That amnesia gag—Now, that was smart! O' course, I reckon any doctor that was up to snuff on all the new ideas would've got wise to you. But me—I'm like the other folks out here. We only know what we read in the papers about things like that. And if a man says he can't remember such and such a thing, it's hard as hell to make a liar out o' him . . . But amnesia don't change a man's character, I reckon. And that's where you slipped up. This thing you're doin' for Starr Landerson—Gary Elliott would never in this world have done a thing like that. That's a grand, generous gesture, and Gary never had a generous thought in all his life. He wasn't built that way."

"Starr's told you, then?"

"She phoned me the minute you hung up. So tickled she could hardly talk. Kept askin' me if I thought you really meant it. Reckon she thought, bein' a doctor, I could read your mind! I can't. If I could, I'd've got wise to you a lot sooner than I did!"

Day shrugged. "It's easy to be generous, if you call it that, with another man's money, Doc. And anyway—"

"Exactly! And that brings us to the second reason that might've brought you here. Whether you killed that Turner girl or not, after Elliott was killed—after you'd made sure he looked more like you than you do yourself—you might've figured that you could take his place for a while, him bein' a comparatively wealthy man, and clean up a quick wad of cash.

A clever man could easily have done it, too . . . But, if that had been your idea, this business of the Star cattle was a made-to-order chance for you. Ninety-odd thousand dollars is a tidy stake, these days. And you could've had it, easy as fallin' off a log. Had it and been gone! But you didn't do it. Instead, you toss off this glorious gesture of yankin' Starr Landerson out of the bogs of debt. What's more, you don't offer to *give* her the money, or lend it to her, neither of which she would've accepted. No! You buy a lot o' worthless land from her, accomplishin' the same result but in a much more graceful way that saves the girl her pride! . . . Doggone it, boy, the more I think of it the more I like the looks of you!"

Day flushed uncomfortably. "Wait, Doc. You're goin' off half-cocked. In the first place, that land ain't worthless. I'm not sayin' Elliott would've bought it. Maybe not. But, when I step out of here, Elliott's heirs won't have any kick comin'. I've bought 'em somethin' worth ten times the value of the Broken Bar. I've bought a dam site and a reservoir. Once that dam is in, there won't be any more drought on the Coronado range. Every acre Elliott owned, and every other acre south of The Notch, will jump in price to ten times what it's valued at today. Water'll make that valley blossom like a rose! And the man that furnishes that water will be, not only a benefactor, but, in time, a millionaire!

"And I've done more than that! I've bought for Elliott's estate some six or seven hundred yards of dirt above the future shore-line of as pretty a lake as a man'll find in the southwest: that reservoir! If they can't make a livin' sellin' water, they can turn that strip above the reservoir into a hotel resort and turn inn-keepers!"

Northup's eyes were twinkling. "So you weren't doin' Starr a favor, after all!" he said. "You'll turn the lower valley into a farmer's paradise and leave poor Starr with nothin' but a cattle ranch!"

"Good God!" Day said explosively. "But *what* a cattle ranch! . . . This business won't injure Starr at all. Every drop of water that Sweetwater Creek brings down from the mountains would feed the upper valley before it ever reached the reservoir. All she needs is a few thousand dollars to build a diversion dam at the north end of the valley and to cut a few irrigation ditches. She could ditch water along the outer edges of that valley down its entire length, if she wanted to, and irrigate the whole damn thing! Or she could water part of it—grow three or four crops of alfalfa on the bottom meadows—and raise the finest beef that ever rode an eastbound freight! Why, damn it, Doc, I'd trade that dam, if it was built, and the Broken Bar, if it was mine, and put my soul in hock besides to own The Star!"

He paused and made a small apologetic gesture with his hands. "I'm sorry," he said. "That's all beside the point."

Northup nodded. "Starr told me you were enthusiastic about it," he said slowly. "And that's another slip. Gary Elliott wouldn't've swapped that car you wrecked for all the land between the Smokies and the Antelopes. Not unless he could sell it, he wouldn't. He hated land. He thought a man who didn't hate it was a hick. Starr noticed that and mentioned it."

Day frowned. "I've wondered at her attitude toward me," he said. "She hated Elliott, didn't she?"

"Well, yes. And no. She couldn't hate *him*, exactly, because she didn't know him. She told me just the other day that she hadn't seen you —Elliott, that is—since he pulled out for school. I didn't know that, but it's easy to see how it could've been that way. Gary was away to school, and later to college, for goin' on eight years. Starr was away four years herself. He spent only one summer here in that time, and that happened to be the summer Starr didn't come home. Then, after Gary finished college, he spent most of his time on the coast; San Francisco, et cetera. Sort of a bright-light playboy, Gary was. Brett Randall, his pal, handled the business for him. Gary made flyin' visits now and then, but him and Starr just happened not to meet . . . What she knew about him was what she heard. And what she heard didn't make her admire him, I reckon. Then, too, he was the man behind the man that was waitin' to take her cattle . . . But she told me she kept findin' things in you that surprised her; nice things; things she didn't look to find in Gary Elliott."

Day said, "Those slips don't matter now." His voice was tired. "I'm caught. The game's played out."

But Northup let that pass. He said, "How did you aim to work it, son? For instance, signin' checks? Or did you aim to pay Starr cash? But even then you'd have to draw it from the bank."

"I thought," Day said, "I'd keep this bandage on my arm. I've found some papers bearin' Elliott's signature. I've practiced it. If I signed a check in front of a man, he'd be pretty apt to take my looks as proof that I was Elliott; and I'd explain any awkwardness or difference in the signature by pointin' out the stiffness in my hand."

He stood up suddenly and crossed the room. A small square table stood beside the bed and Northup heard a drawer creak open and slide shut as Day bent over it.

There was a gun in that drawer; a small, flat, ugly automatic gun like the one Gary Elliott had had that night in Wigwam Gap. Day looked at it while Northup's voice went on.

"Yes, that would work, I reckon . . . But this dam idea of yours—a thing like that would cost a pile of money. How'd you figure to finance it, Day? Or did you plan that far ahead?"

Day did not turn. "Elliott was a millionaire, wasn't he? I reckon his heirs won't find it hard to swing a dam."

"He wasn't though. T. J. Elliott, Gary's Dad, was worth some millions when he died, all right; but Gary was a gambler. The stock market got him, see? Cleaned him out! About all Gary had was this ranch; and he'd've sold that, I reckon, if he could've found a buyer in times like these. He needed cash to keep the bright light flickerin'. That's why I said he never would've done this thing for Starr . . . Oh, well! That part of it needn't worry you, eh? You've acquired a damn valuable piece of property for Gary's heirs, providin' he's got any heirs. Let them figure out a way to make it pay, eh? Your little masquerade ain't apt to last that long, I reckon, anyway."

Day turned, the gun held loosely in his hand. But Northup did not see. Northup's eyes were closed his shaggy head tipped back against the wall, and he was smiling thoughtfully.

"And that reminds me!" Lary said softly. Something in his voice brought Northup's head erect. "I aim," Day said, "to see this one deal through! Sit steady, Doc! The pills in this pop-gun are small, but mighty poisonous!"

Northup blinked with round-eyed wonder at the gun. His jaw sagged down. "Good God-a'mighty, son!" he barked. "Put up that gun! What's wrong with you?"

"It just occurs to me," Day said, "that I will need a car. Your car! You see, my deal with

Starr ain't finished yet. So, Doc, that's your hard luck!"

Northup stared at him. "What do you mean?"

"Just this: I'm goin' to phone Starr. Have her meet me in town. Those cows are worth ninety-odd thousand, Randall said. There's close to twenty thousand in Elliott's checkin' account. I'm goin' to give Starr a bill of sale for those cows, plus my check for sixteen thousand, in return for a quit-claim deed to that land! That way I figure it, once this deal is made it won't be broken, even when it's proved that I had no right to make it. Starr won't break it, because she needs the money. Elliott's heirs won't break it, because this drought has taught 'em that they need that dam. On the other hand, if I *don't* complete the deal, it'll take some time to settle Elliott's estate and, even if his hcirs wanted to buy that land and build a dam, Starr would've lost her ranch by then and wouldn't benefit . . . So, Doc, I'll have to tie you up. I'll lock you in a closet here and I'll take Chang along with me. He needs to buy some groceries, anyway. It's not yet noon. With luck, Chang should be back by dark. Of course, somebody may drop in and turn you loose before that time. I'll have to take a chance on that . . . Stand up and face the wall."

But, for a moment, Northup did not move. Then, suddenly, he laughed. His head tipped back, his shoulders heaved, and his big voice rolled out in a Gargantuan mirth. Day stared at him.

Long moments passed before that laughter ceased. Then Northup lurched erect, red faced and choking, and reached out to shove Day's gun aside.

"You fool!" he gasped. "You damn young fool!"

Day said, bewilderedly, "I reckon so. But why?"

Somehow the doctor's laughter had disheartened him. A moment ago his scheme had seemed entirely plausible. Make Northup a prisoner; get to town; complete the purchase of the land, and then—escape. It had not seemed too difficult.

But now . . . There must be some transparent flaw in the plan that he had failed to see. Perhaps Northup had already exposed him. Perhaps a trap was set already, waiting to be sprung.

As if to verify his fears, Chang's flute-like

voice came through an open door. "Beg pa'don, boss. Men come. Shel'f Marsden say you come and talk with him chop-chop."

Day's gaze swept back to Northup's face. "You didn't waste much time!" he said.

But Northup's face was blank. Day heard the jingling thud of spurred heels on the porch. He said, evenly, "You'd better beat it, Doc. I'll make a fight. I'd rather take a bullet than a rope."

Then Northup found his voice explosively. "No, damn it! Listen, son! I didn't bring Lem Marsden here! I'm backin' *you!* This thing you're doin' for Starr Landerson is too damn good to spoil! I love that girl; and, damn it, I like you! . . . I'm bettin' this is just coincidence; that Marsden don't know who you are. He can't know! Nobody knew but me. And I ain't so sure but what you're kiddin' *me!*"

He grinned. Day stared at him. "But how about that broken arm?" Day said.

"To hell with that! Come t' think of it, I ain't so sure about that arm as I thought I was. Maybe it was one o' them Gillespie kids. Good God-a'mighty, boy, I've set a *thousand* broken arms! I can't remember all o' them!"

Day grinned. "Okay," he said. "I'll take your

word." His hand shot out and Northup gripped it heartily. "Look out for Marsden, son," he said. "Him and Elliott were pretty thick. I don't know why. But—watch your step!"

10

DR. JASON NORTHUP said, "Gary, this is Brett Randall, your friend. And this is Lemuel Marsden, sheriff of Coronado county."

He turned to face the visitors and made a small apologetic shrug. "Seems odd, I reckon, to have to introduce you men. But Gary's had a blow on the head that has wiped out his memory."

Beneath his disapproving brows he watched them as they greeted Day. Brett Randall, bald, hawk-beaked, a lean man gone to belly underneath his belt, shook hands and murmured the amenities. "He's like a vulture," Northup thought, and liked the simile. Loose flesh formed wattles under Randall's jowls and the bald head slanting back above black bushy brows bore out the similarity. Northup felt a vague uneasiness at finding Randall here. Lem Marsden was a far more dangerous-seeming man, but Northup thought, "Where ever Randall is, there's a carcass to be picked! I hope the kid don't concentrate on Marsden's ugly looks and underestimate Brett Randall's brains!"

Lem Marsden grunted and sat down. "We'd like t' talk t' you, Elliott," he said. "Alone!"

There was something like a threat in Marsden's tone and in the bleak, unfriendly glance at Northup that accompanied it.

The doctor shrugged. "I'm leavin'," he said curtly. He turned to Day. "Keep working on that hand, Gary. An hour's massage every day will work the stiffness out of those tendons better than anything I could do for you would do. But you'll have to keep at it. A thing like that is slow to heal."

Day nodded understandingly. Northup was giving him a lead to cover any question that might arise concerning a disparity of signatures. Day thought, "He's trustin' me a damn long way! With that remark to cover me, I could cash in on Elliott's entire estate!"

There was a silence then while Northup ambled to his car. Brett Randall turned his back to Day, lighting a cigar as he watched Northup's car swing down the drive. The pause gave Lary time to weigh the men he had to face. He disliked Randall, both from hearsay and from sight, instinctively. But he found it hard to make an estimate of him. Lem Marsden was less difficult to understand. There was nothing subtle about Marsden. He was a burly man, rawboned and obviously dangerous. His skin and features showed a trace of Indian blood, Day thought. He wore a vest, unbuttoned, with a holstered gun beneath his right armpit. Day noted that. It made him conscious of the pressure against his ribs of the flat, black automatic he had hidden there after threatening Northup a while ago.

Marsden's bleak gaze swung to Day as Randall turned. "What's this damn foolishness about your not rememberin' us?"

"It's called amnesia," Day said. "It's right embarrassin', not bein' able to identify your—friends."

The little pause between the words was challenging. Lem Marsden's voice picked up the glove. "It don't keep yuh from rememberin' how t' doublecross your friends, though, does it, Elliott?"

Day's nerves were taut. He said, "I don't know what you mean."

"Don't lie!" Lem Marsden's hands raked, talonlike, along his thighs as he lunged forward in his chair. His sudden violence was startling. Day froze, alert to meet a physical attack. But Randall intervened.

"Wait, Lem." Randall's suave, ingratiating smile plowed new and even uglier furrows in his face. "I'm sure this thing can all be handled —diplomatically. Eh, Gary? Between friends, so to speak."

"There seems to be some doubt," Day said, "about our bein' friends."

Randall made a small deprecating gesture with his hands. "Don't let Lem's little outburst —mislead you, Gary. Lem is naturally— impulsive."

Randall's jerky mode of speech was vaguely irritating. He paused and swallowed between words, the adam's apple jerking in his scrawny throat.

Day frowned. "Get on with it," he said impatiently.

Randall leaned forward a little, his eyes narrowing, and for the first time Lary felt the patent possibilities behind the gambler's pious mask. Those narrowed eyes were shrewd and hard.

"We came to ask if it is true that you're negotiating with Miss Landerson for the purchase of Star Valley, or for part of it."

There was no break in Randall's speech this time. The words came fluently, almost purring in their even flow. A warning rang somewhere in Lary's brain. He said, "How'd you know that?"

Lem Marsden leered and nodded as he sat back in his chair. But it was Randall who answered Day's question. "It's—my business, more or less, to keep—informed on things like that. One of the young ladies at the telephone exchange is a friend of mine. Naturally, a call from you to Miss Landerson comes under the head of news! She—listened in."

Day said, "I see! Well, that's worth knowin', anyway. All right. Go on from there."

"Then it's true," Marsden said smoothly, "that you're offering Miss Landerson a rather —remarkable—sum for certain lands?"

"It's true," Day said, "that I'm buyin' land from her. Whether the price is remarkable or not is a matter of opinion. I'm payin' what I think it's worth."

Brett Randall nodded. "The question is," he said, "why do you think it's worth so much?"

Day grinned. "That reminds me of a thing

we used to say when we was kids. 'That's for me to know and you to find out!'"

That small defiance struck with unexpected force. Lem Marsden's growl was wolflike, inarticulate. But it was Randall whose reaction puzzled Day. Randall's jaw sagged comically, his face a picture of surprise and doubt. But doubt gave way before the evidence he saw in Lary's face. He nodded finally.

"Now that," he said, "comes nearer than Doc Northup did to convincing me about this —what's its name?—amnesia! you really think that I don't know!"

And, suddenly, Day understood. He thought, "So Gary Elliott was in cahoots with him to get The Star!" The knowledge startled him. He saw more clearly now than he had seen before what treacherous ground he stood upon; how one apparently innocuous word might ruin him. But his voice was even when he spoke again. He said, "I don't quite sabe that. I may be dumb."

Brett Randall grinned. "If you don't know that I'm already aware of the—ah—peculiar value of that land, your memory is, indeed, impaired! Because we went into that, Gary, quite thoroughly, a year ago!"

He paused and frowned. "But there's a flaw

in that. If you've—forgotten so much, what was your object in buying the land? You would have forgotten *that*, too." He shook his head. "No, Gary. I'm afraid it won't go down! You're not so dumb, after all!"

Marsden grunted impatiently. "Hell!" he said. "A man don't need t' be so damn smart t' know that Star Valley is worth a damn sight more than what he's paying for it. Get to the point, why don't you?"

"The point being," Lary said, "that my buyin' the land prevents you, Randall, from foreclosin' on it."

But Randall let that pass. When he spoke, it was to answer Marsden; but his beady eyes were fixed on Day, and once again his speech was fluent, smooth. "The point is, Gary isn't buying *all* The Star. In fact, he's buying only that part of the valley south of a line marked roughly by the summit of the rocky slope above The Notch."

This time, it was Lem Marsden's face on which amazement made a comic mask. That fact registered on Lary's mind. Marsden, then, had not known all the facts.

But Randall's voice flowed on. "The point is, Gary's paying a high price for a lot of rocky, worthless ground ... Worthless, that is, unless—"

"Unless a man intends to build a dam," Day said. "Your lady friend seems to have given you the dope quite accurately. If you know that much, the secret's out. All right. I aim to build a dam!"

"A dam, eh? To irrigate the Coronado range." Randall sat back, smiling, nodding skeptically. "So that's your—story, eh? Matt Landerson's old dream! ... Well, suppose we —agree—that that's your reason. To cash in on it properly, you ought to buy up all you can of Coronado range. A scheme like that takes money. It takes time. Millions; years. It would take shrewd dealing, too. That's not your type of game. You've always wanted ready cash ... I'll—buy your bargain, eh? The deal is not— completed, I understand? All right! What would you take to—let the matter drop?"

Day grinned. "And let you foreclose your skinflint mortgage?" He shook his head. "You men can't deal with me. You're wastin' time."

This time, Brett Randall's voice was harsh. "I didn't think we could!" he said. "I'll tell you why! Because it ain't the irrigation scheme you're playin' for! Not that at all! That's just a bluff!"

He paused abruptly and Day prompted him. "Go on! You said you'd tell me why I'm buyin' it."

But Randall hedged. He opened his lips as if to speak; thought better of it; gulped, and shook his head. His face was purple now with pent-up rage. Lem Marsden glanced at him and then at Day.

"We'll deal," Lem Marsden said.

The very softness of his voice was startling. The lack of bluster made the man seem more than ever dangerous. Day turned to face him, warily.

"You deal and like it, Elliott!" Lem Marsden grinned. "Randall's offered t' play ball with yuh. I'm not so generous! I've got yuh where the hair is short, sabe? You'll deal with me, or else!"

Brett Randall raised his hand as if to interfere again, then shrugged and dropped back in his chair. That withdrawal in itself was eloquent. It seemed to mean diplomacy has failed. The time has come to make a show of force. Enter —the fighting man!

"Not very long ago," Lem Marsden said, "I

got a telegram. It was from a man named Blaine. Blaine is the sheriff of Sedalia County, in case your memory's as bad as you say it is! . . . I got that telegram here now."

Day's heart thumped heavily and then slowed down. He was alert and tense, yet strangely cool. He thought, "So it's to be a showdown after all! Then why all this preliminary talk?"

He hooked both thumbs into his belt. The fingers of his left hand reached within two inches of the gun he carried there. Gary Elliott's gun. He wondered just how fast Lem Marsden's big hands were. It would be Marsden's left hand that would shoot toward the holstered gun if Marsden drew. Day thought, "I must remember that."

He felt Brett Randall's eyes upon him and knew that he must keep his face expressionless. And that was hard. It seemed a long, long time before Lem Marsden drew a yellow paper from his vest and flattened it.

"This thing is dated August 12th," Marsden said. "Here's what it says:"

PLEASE COMPARE PICTURES OF LARY DAY, RODEO PERFORMER WITH MAN NAMED GARY, LAST

NAME UNKNOWN, OF CORONADO STOP A MISS STARR LANDERSON IS SAID TO HAVE MISTAKEN DAY FOR GARY STOP DAY ON TRIAL FOR MURDER OF BELLE TURNER IN SEDALIA NIGHT OF JULY THIRD STOP WIRE ANSWER.

As Marsden finished reading he looked up and grinned. Day met his gaze. "So what?" he said.

"So I covered you, Elliott! I found them pictures, and this Lary Day looks more like you than you do yourself! Same face, same size, same colorin', same everything! . . . But I told Blaine different, see? I told him the resemblance was only slight. I even went further than that. I told him that you had an alibi for the night of July third; that I could vouch for it . . . And you didn't, Elliott; I took pains to look that up!"

There was a pause. Day said, "Then why'd you lie?"

In spite of his effort to be calm, his voice rasped with an eagerness he could not hide. His heart was pounding now unchecked. This was the thing that he had come to do; to wreck that alibi of Elliott's. Here was success where he had feared defeat!

Lem Marsden grinned. "Maybe it was because I was a friend o' yours. Or maybe I figured you'd make it worth my while. No matter why. I've got the whiphand *now*! You sabe that, don't you? With this thing hangin' over you, I reckon you'll behave!"

Day took a long deep breath. He dared not glance at Randall now, but he could feel the gambler's probing eyes. He held his voice to steadiness. "So you believe that I'm the man who killed the Turner girl," he said. "That Day was innocent. That it?"

Lem Marsden grinned. "I ain't sayin' you killed her. All I'm sayin' is, you've got no alibi. Not that I know of, you ain't. You wasn't here, that's sure. Vale told me that. About noon on the second of July you headed north in that big car o' yours. Maybe you went to Sedalia. Maybe you didn't. But early in the mornin' of the Fourth you come down from the north and stopped for breakfast at that fillin' station where the Coronado road forks east. And you was tuckered out. Jumpy. Nerves on edge. Hank Green, the man that runs the fillin' station, told me that . . . What's more, this Turner girl lived in San Francisco. You've spent a lot o' time in Frisco these past two years. You might've met her there . . . No, I ain't sayin' you killed her, Elliott. But I'm bettin' you ain't hankerin' t' have t' go t' court and *prove* you didn't! I figured you'd rather deal with us than that!"

"I see." Day spoke very carefully now. "But here's a thing you seem to overlook. I don't know what the hell you're drivin' at. Sure, I can see where Randall's sore because this deal of mine prevents him from foreclosin' on The Star. But aside from that, I'm in the dark. And as to this Belle Turner thing—my memory doesn't reach beyond that wreck, ten days ago."

Lem Marsden interrupted him. "If that's the truth, you're in a damn sight tighter spot! A murder trial would be downright embarrassin', by God, for a man who couldn't remember where he was, or where he was supposed t' be, or even whether he was innocent or not!"

Day grinned. "That's true. But, on the other hand, it makes me harder to stampede. If I could remember, it's possible that I might have somethin' to conceal. Or if you men could prove that I had anything to do with it . . ."

He paused deliberately to let that hint sink home.

"But, as it is—" He shrugged. "The mere fact that I happened to look like this what's-his-name—this Lary Day—and that I was away from home the night he killed this Turner girl—That's too damn thin!"

Lem Marsden gulped. This deadlock left him at a loss. Day turned to meet Brett Randall's beady eyes. The gambler shrugged. "You're—sure—that that's your last word, Elliott?"

Day's grin was impudent. "It seems to me," he said, "that it's your move!"

Brett Randall nodded jerkily. "We'll move, all right!" he snapped. "Come, Marsden. We've no further business here."

Lem Marsden followed Randall like a surly dog, unwilling but obedient; and Day stood watching them until their car rolled out of sight along the twisting trail. The thrill of victory ran through him like a heady wine, exhilarating him. For it had been a victory; a test that he had met and passed. He had distinctly scored against Brett Randall and his fighting man. Just how he had defeated them, he did not know. Brett Randall wanted Star Valley. That much was obvious and natural. But there were undercurrents here that Day could feel but could not understand. Randall's defeat lay deeper than the mere frustration of his desire to own The Star. It was The Notch itself that Randall coveted; The Notch and that bleak land adjoining it. But why?

"It's not the irrigation scheme," Day thought. "Randall knew about that, but it was secondary in his mind. It's somethin' else. Just what, I'd give a pretty to find out!"

At any rate, his own affairs had definitely progressed. Gary Elliott's alibi was no longer an alibi. The identical appearance of Elliott and Day, combined with the possibility of Elliott's presence in Sedalia on the night of the crime, provided ground for doubt of Lary's guilt to say the least. And a reasonable doubt, based on new evidence, would be sufficient cause for a new trial. Lem Marsden would be an unwilling witness, of course; but Red Vale and Chang and the Greens, Henry and Sarah, would provide the needed testimony. Too, Northup and Starr Landerson would serve as witnesses.

That thought of Chang was like a rub upon the genie's lamp. His clear, melodious voice cut through Day's revery. "Dinner get cold. You come now, boss?"

Day turned to meet Chang's bland, inquiring gaze. He wondered how long Chang had stood there, just inside that door. "You might've said that earlier, Chang," he said. "Not very hospitable, sendin' Randall and the sheriff off at mealtime, eh? I never thought of it, myself."

Chang blinked. "No good," he said. "Bad men! More better they go hungly, eh? To hell with them!"

And Lary laughed delightedly. It was the longest speech that he had ever heard Chang make, and the most human one. And, in a way, it answered his unspoken thought. Chang had heard enough, at least, to place the visitors as enemies.

It was the third surprise of what had been, so far, a highly satisfactory day.

11

BUT Lem Marsden and Brett Randall, riding down toward Coronado after their not quite conclusive interview with Day, were in no such a self-complacent mood.

Marsden clutched desperately at the door as the car lurched down the steep, rocky slope toward the pavement where the wreckage of Gary Elliott's big yellow roadster still made a splotch of color against the foot of the opposite bank. He relaxed a little as the car settled to the smoother going, but the glance he turned on Randall was a scowling one.

"What was the idea, Brett, of holdin' out on me?"

Brett Randall grunted. "Just how," he said, "have I held out on you?"

"You told me Elliott was liftin' the mortgage on The Star. I figured that meant he was buyin' a half-interest in the outfit, or somethin' like that. Now it turns out that all he's buyin' is The Notch and that no-'count land at the south end o' the Valley."

Randall shrugged. "The result is the same, isn't it? If the deal goes through, Starr Landerson will pay off the mortgage and my last hold on The Star will go glimmering."

"Yeah. But, Brett, I've done a lot o' dirty work for you. Seems like you ought t' trust me more. You take today. Right from the start, I was goin' in the dark. I might've balled things up."

Randall chuckled. "You did right well!" he said. "That telegram, for instance—"

"Well, thanks. But what I'm drivin' at is this: What's Gary want with that damn land, anyway? It won't even graze sheep! And he's payin' high for it; damn high. Now, why?"

"He told you why," Randall growled. "He aims to build a dam!"

"Like hell he does! That was a bluff. But you know the real reason, Brett. Fact is, from the way you talked I got the idea that his reason for buyin' that land was your reason for wantin' The Star."

"That's right. It is!"

"But, hell! That don't make sense! I thought—"

"That's where you made your mistake," Randall said curtly. "You're all right, Lem. As a range boss, or as a fighting man, you'll do real well. That's why I promised you the running of The Star. But when it comes to thinking, Lem, leave that to me. It's not exactly in your line."

They drove in silence for a mile or more. Marsden framed a tart rejoinder in his mind; thought better of it and sat gloomily, shooting sidelong glances at the man behind the steering wheel. That Randall, given time enough, would talk, Lem Marsden knew. He had to talk. For, now that Marsden had scented mystery, that mystery had to be explained. They had worked together much too long to split up now, and Randall was too shrewd to hope that Marsden would go further than he had already gone upon a course he could not see.

But when Randall spoke at last it was as if he talked unwillingly, obedient to some inner compulsion that was distasteful to him.

"All my life," Brett Randall said, "I've fought for wealth; worked for it; prayed for it! And it's avoided me. Oh, yes, I know Coronado thinks I'm rich. I've got money enough for common comforts, yes. But wealth—power—that's avoided me."

His hands upon the steering wheel gripped

hard until the knuckles stood out white as pearl against the blotched, dark skin.

"And T. J. Elliott was a millionaire!" He filled the words with bitterness. "T. J. Elliott was a cattleman. There's no tougher game—no longer odds—in all the world, I reckon, than prospecting for gold. Or copper. And T. J. Elliott knew not one damn thing about the game . . . And yet he made a fortune out of it! . . . I spend my life, slaving at a game I really know, for what? Comparatively, I'm poor! And Elliott stumbles on a copper mine by luck; blind, crazy luck! Made millions out of it—for that fool son of his to throw away!"

The passion in Brett Randall's voice made Marsden glance at him. There was a pause. Randall's hands upon the wheel relaxed their grip. His voice was calmer when he spoke again.

"I reckon that's the biggest thrill there is—finding a fortune in the ground. Once Elliott had tasted it, he wanted more. It wasn't the money, so much. He had more money than he had brains to use, already. But it was the thrill he was after . . . He kept on takin' claims. He grub-staked enough prospectors to fill a good-sized town. . . . They say lightning never strikes twice in the same place. But, for T. J. Elliott, it did!"

"You mean he struck it right again? I never heard o' that."

"Few people did . . . A few months before he died, T. J. Elliott made a final attempt to buy Star Valley. He boosted his price considerably above his best previous offer. But I didn't think anything of that because, next to his passion for prospecting, Elliott coveted The Star. He wanted Star Valley worse, I reckon, than he ever wanted anything he couldn't get. . . . But Matt Landerson said no. Matt Landerson loved that land himself.

"Well, T. J. died and Gary started out to buck the Wall Street boys. He hit the market all spraddled out just about the time the bottom dropped out of it. He lost his shirt! I told him to take his licking and get out, but no! He fought the avalanche! He dropped two million dollars in two months."

Lem Marsden whistled an incredulous, awe-stricken note. But Randall seemed not to hear.

"Oh, Gary wasn't broke, exactly. He still had enough to play the good-time sucker to a lot of bright-light tarts; enough to sneer at work and let a million-dollar outfit like the Broken Bar go plumb to hell! But he was scared, all right. Money'd always come so easy in his life, I reckon he thought it grew on trees! And he was damn near right. He had the Elliott luck.

"Things went on until not quite a year ago. And then I found out why T. J. Elliott had made that last stab at buying The Star. Gary came to me one day, half crazy with the same idea. He wanted to borrow money—he didn't care how much; a million, or two million, any amount. At first, he wouldn't tell me why. But finally I got it out of him. A while before he died, T. J. had struck a gold mine. He'd had some samples analyzed by some west-coast mining outfit and, while they weren't rich, they were good pay dirt. T. J. then had some mining engineers send men out here—all on the quiet, you understand—to examine the prospect. They made borings to determine the direction and probable extent of the vein. On the basis of their report the mining outfit wound up by offering T. J. a half million dollars cash for mining privileges and a controlling interest. . . . And just about that time, T. J. found out that he didn't own the claim! He thought he'd staked on the public domain. But when he came to checkin' the surveys he learned that his gold mine belonged to old Matt Landerson!"

"The hell!" Lem Marsden was excited now. "But how'd he make a mistake like that? He knew Landerson owned all o' Star Valley. How'd he come t' go prospectin' in there?"

"Landerson owned outside the Valley, too. You didn't know that, did you? I didn't know it. T. J. didn't know it. But it's true. . . . So then I knew why T. J. had boosted his offer. . . . Landerson still wouldn't sell, so T. J. sat tight; refused the mining company's offer and said nothing. And died. . . . Then the price of gold began to climb. The mining outfits began to look for sources of supply. The particular mining company T. J. had approached remembered him. They wrote Gary, doubling their original offer! A cool million! . . . And gold is still soaring! Why, man, no telling what that claim is worth!"

Brett Randall wiped a film of sweat from his cold brow. Lem Marsden gulped. "And that girl owns it! And don't know it's there!"

"Exactly! . . . I knew that Starr Landerson would never sell. But—I knew, too, that she was in a jam—or could be *put* in one. So I bought the mortgage against The Star and demanded a fifty-percent reduction of the principal. That took a hundred thousand dollars, and Starr Landerson didn't have a tenth of that. She tried to raise it but loan money nowadays is suspicious of grange security.

"So—I made Gary Elliott scrape up a hundred thousand dollars, lend it to Starr Landerson and take a mortgage on her stock. I might've foreclosed then, since the mortgage was due; but I was afraid she might be able somehow to scrape together enough cash to pay it off. The beef market wasn't as bad then as it is now, and while a foreclosure then would have ruined her, she might have saved the land. I played it safe. I knew if she lost her cattle she was licked, and licked right. . . . I acted for Gary in making the loan against the stock. Starr didn't know, at first, that the money was coming from Gary Elliott, but she was scared and willing to take the loan from where she could get it. I fixed the appraisal so it took every cow she owned to stand security against the debt. She kicked but there was nothing she could really do."

Lem Marsden nodded knowingly. "I get it!" he said. "After that, you set back and prayed that the beef market would go to hell and that all Star-branded cows would drop their calves stillborn!"

Randall shrugged. "I did better than that! I couldn't control the market, and I have damned little faith in prayer. But there was one thing I could do, and did. I made Gary Elliott hire a new range boss!"

"Red Vale!" Lem Marsden breathed.

"Red Vale! Exactly!"

"So that's why you kept hintin' that it wouldn't be smart for me to work too hard runnin' down the facts about this recent rustlin', eh?"

"You wanted the job of running The Star, didn't you?" Brett Randall grinned.

"You're damned right I did! Man, that's the sweetest cattle country in the world! . . . But I didn't see, then, that this sudden epidemic of cow-stealin' was helpin' me to get that job!"

"It was, though. I don't know how many head of Star cattle Vale got away with but, judging by the tally I got yesterday on what was left of The Star herds, it must've been plenty! He doublecrossed us some, but I expected that. I mean, he's rustled some stuff other than from The Star. That's what caused the kick you heard. But otherwise, he did a damn good job."

"You mean you turned Vale loose? Let him rustle all he could get away with? Why hell! Short-handed as The Star has been, he might've stripped 'em clean."

"He wasn't turned loose, exactly. Gary kept a check on him; or rather, I did. Gary wasn't here enough to do so very much. But Vale was working for Gary, you see. Vale was to get so much a head for every head he stole. But, of course, if Vale carried it too far, Gary stood to lose by it when he foreclosed. Besides, Vale was limited by the drought. In ordinary times, a man could graze an almost unlimited number of cattle in the hills, in any one of the hundred hidden parks. But the drought changed that. Grass is scarce up there now, and so is water. Vale found a place, I don't know where, that had grass and water for a certain number of cows. But when he got that many he had to stop. You see, they had to hold the stuff until Gary foreclosed his mortgage. Oh, the brands could have been worked, I suppose; or the cattle could have been peddled to some buyer who would close his eyes to the fact that they were stolen. But that would mean selling at a price far below the market, and it would entail a big element of risk. It was simpler to wait until Gary took legal possession of the Star herds. After that, he could sell all Star-branded stock he might happen to have, and no questions asked. . . . The main thing is, Vale got enough so that there was no chance of Starr Landerson's being able to meet that mortgage."

"Seems to me you overlooked a bet, though, in not gettin' yourself a share o' them cattle," Marsden said.

Randall grinned. "That was chicken feed, Lem! I stood to get The Star, you see. And I stood to get the mine. My agreement with Gary was that he would get whatever cash the mine might bring as payment for his rather tenuous claim as heir to the discoverer, and I was to get the forty-nine percent interest not sold to the mining company." Randall smiled thoughtfully. "Of course, Gary might possibly have had difficulty in—collecting—on that agreement! Once I had foreclosed and gained title to the property, Gary would have been dependent on my—generosity—as to the extent of his share. However, that's beside the point."

Marsden chuckled. "I got a swell picture o' what Gary would've got! He was pretty dumb, givin' you the whiphand like he done."

Randall smiled complacently. "Gary thought,

you see, that *he* had the whiphand. He thought his knowledge of the location of the claim gave him that. The mining company didn't know exactly where the claim was or they would have found the real owner from the deeds. Gary never *told* me, you see, that the mining engineers had a record of the location. They couldn't have made a report that would have impressed the mining company without a thorough investigation. So I left Gary's mind at rest. But I made some inquiries—careful ones—and found out that the investigations had been made. The engineers weren't interested in the real owners of the land; they'd done their job and had been paid for it. So then I knew that the location of the mine was no secret."

Marsden nodded. "Just the same, I hate to think of all them cattle slippin' through our hands. They ain't worth so much right now, maybe, but this drought is bound to force the price o' beef sky-high."

"I think you're right. Fortunately, the upward swing didn't come in time to upset our plans. Everything worked out perfectly. Elliott's foreclosure went through; it's less than ninety days until my mortgage on The Star falls due. It's in the bag—except for one damn thing! Elliott is doublecrossing me!"

Marsden nodded. "Now, why d'you reckon he's doin' that, Brett? What's it gettin' him to cut you out? He'll have to split with the girl, this way; that's the only difference. Looks like he'd just as lief go on through with it like you planned, with you. . . . Or maybe he's got wise t' himself and doped it out that you ain't aimin' to give him his split."

Randall's answer was a snarl. "Split, nothing! God almighty, Lem, don't be so dumb! This way, he won't have to split with anybody! *He's bought the mine! All* of it, you understand. The whole damn thing!"

It took a moment for that fact to penetrate. Marsden nodded finally. "I get it! The mine's in the south end o' the Valley, is that it? Somewhere on that rocky slope above The Notch. . . ."

"No!" Randall's voice shrilled up. "Not on that slope! And Elliott isn't buying just the south end of Star Valley. He's buying all Landerson land south of a given point. That point happens to be at the top of that slope; but that's just a blind, just camouflage. He's telling Starr Landerson that he intends to build an irrigation dam and he's buying the reservoir site along with what he really wants so she won't smell a rat. The mine is in the ridge just west of The Notch. T. J. Elliott—and everybody else, I reckon, including myself—had always supposed that ridge was public property. It's worthless, apparently. Nobody cared. But it belonged to Landerson. Matt Landerson, and Matt's Dad before him, always dreamed of damming Sweetwater Creek at The Notch to irrigate the Coronado range. So one of them, years ago, bought land on either side of The Notch to protect the site of that proposed dam. And that's what Gary Elliott is buying! He's not only getting the mine, but he's enabling Starr Landerson to pay off her mortage so I'll never own The Star!"

Marsden spent a moment in deep, scowling thought. "But how the hell did he figure out that if he can't *remember* anything? Seems like he'd've forgot the whole damn thing, the mine and all."

"Forgotten? Hell! That gag about his memory is—rot! He's faking it! But he's shrewd. He almost got away with that amnesia stuff; had me half-way convinced: Until you sprung that telegram! That jarred him! I saw it in his face!"

Marsden nodded. "Yeah, that got him where he wasn't expectin' it! . . . But it don't help much. He's froze you out, looks like. It's too damn bad!"

Brett Randall wrenched the car around a curve. Marsden reached out hurriedly to clutch the door again. "Not yet, by God!" Brett Randall said. "I'm not licked yet! There's one thing you've forgotten, Lem!"

"What's that?"

"The deal is not complete! And won't be for a while. It'll take a month or more to make the necessary surveys and to have the title searched. Gary's buying an option on that land, figuring to take the rise in the beef market on those Star cattle to get the cash to swing the deal. A sixty-day option. Two months. And in two months, things might just possibly occur!"

"Such as?"

"We might find proof that Gary killed that Turner girl. He might've, you know. As far as we know, he had the opportunity. And she was just the kind of a little tart he liked to strut before. Whether he actually killed her or not, one thing I'm certain of. There's something in that business that frightens him!"

Marsden nodded thoughtfully. "We can do some probin' there, all right. If he really killed her, we got him hooked! With murder hangin' over him, he'd see the light! . . . But it's a damn long shot."

"There's still another possibility," Brett Randall said, "if that one fails. If Gary was to —die—before that deal was completed. . . ."

He paused. The racket of the car took on a wailing overtone as Randall's nerves grew taut and forced his foot down gradually, and further down, against the floor.

Lem Marsden glanced at him. He cleared his throat. "The second way's the surest, and the easiest," he said. "I'll tend to it."

12

DROUGHT lay upon the Coronado range like a gigantic leech. It sucked the life-blood from the land. It dried the streams. It turned a pleasant grazing land into an arid gridiron, blackened and inhospitable. Even Sweetwater Creek, in normal times a never-failing artery, was empty now for more than half its length below The Notch, and its tributary streams turned dusty beds, like bleaching bones, up to a red unfriendly sun.

As other water sources failed, cattle had come down from the outlying ranges to graze along the diminishing length of Sweetwater. But grass soon failed them there as it had failed them everywhere. Hoofs and hunger wore the land to nakedness so that the trek from grass to water, back to grass again, became an endless, lengthening round.

Lean cattle, mournful-eyed, their muzzles pierced with cactus spines as mute and bloody evidence of the resorts to which their hunger had driven them, filled Starr with pity as her car rolled through The Notch toward the town of Coronado on her way to keep her promise to Lary Day. Some sixteen months had passed since rain in any quantity had washed this thirsty land. Even the winter snowfall on the peaks had failed. Month after month the Smokies and the Antelopes had thrust their summits, blue, unblanketed, against a leaden sky and, month by month, farm folk and cattle folk alike had whistled to keep up their hope of a wet spring. But spring had come and gone and merely added heat to other woes. Heat that parched the scanty grass and withered it. Dry, sucking heat, day after day.

Star Valley was the only Mecca now in all this wilderness. The subterranean flow from the surrounding slopes had kept it fairly moist long after the lower range was dry, and its deep soil had held the moisture with a stubborn thrift. Too, Sweetwater Creek diminished less rapidly than it had done in the spongy soil below The Notch.

But it was poverty, almost as much as wealth of natural resources, that had contributed toward the Valley's stubborn vitality. The range was understocked. Starr Landerson's depleted herds lacked the numbers to wreak such havoc on the stronger range as that achieved by the massed herds below The Notch. Old Tom McElvey, major domo and general factotum of Star Valley since before its present owner's advent there, had prophesied the drought and, in the first summer of its existence, had held the Star herds up along the timbered slopes long after they would ordinarily have drifted down upon the Valley range. That foresight had preserved the grass remarkably. So much so that, when Gary Elliott's foreclosure struck the final doom of the Star herds, the cattle were graded by prospective purchasers as fat prime beef on a market glutted with the gaunt tough victims of the drought.

And it was old McElvey's boast that he could have carried the Star cattle through still another year or more of drought and kept them fat. He would still have water, for he was convinced that Sweetwater above The Notch would never fail. And he still had stacks and stacks of sweet, cured, valley hay. For twenty years it had been his, McElvey's, and Matt Landerson's unfailing policy to cut and stack as much good feed as they could easily handle and those long lines of stacks, fenced carefully against the stock, had increased annually, almost untouched. They were Star's reserve against a rainless day; and even now, after so many such days, those stacks still stood.

Would stand, perhaps, indefinitely. For now there were no herds. Two hundred head or so of saddle stock, a cowhide chair or two, some wagons, and the bunkhouse door—those things and those alone now bore the Landerson Star brand as mark of ownership.

So that Star Valley, too, was desolate. It was not the same desolation that lay upon the lower Coronado range, but it was a desolation quite as potent, quite as ruinous. The Star had water, grass and stacks of hay, but no cattle. The lower range had none of these except the cattle. And, except perhaps for Gary Elliott, no one on the lower range had money wherewith to buy the plenty that the Star had to offer.

Gary Elliott, then, was The Star's one and only hope. How desperate a hope, Starr dared not let herself admit, because she loved the Valley with a deep and jealous love. The very roots of her existence were sunk deep into that soil. On a grassy knoll just east of the big, rambling old ranch-house in which she had been born, a line of graves beneath tall pines bore headboard markings on which, deep-chiseled, stood the record of her clan. Still other graves, a bit apart from these, held men whose lives had been poured out into the land; tall riders who had helped to build and hold The Star. Such ties grip hard, and so Starr Landerson was bound. But they were pleasant bonds, made easy by her own affection for the land. To lose The Star would leave her derelict.

If Gary Elliott carried out his promise to purchase the southern tip of the Valley at a highly satisfactory price—land The Star could comfortably spare—then there was hope. That sale, coupled with Elliott's further proposal to rent The Star as grazing ground for his newly acquired herds, would lift the mortgage held by Randall and leave a margin with which to start the long slow climb back to prosperity. It would be a slender margin, certainly. But it would serve.

"And he will go through with it," Starr told herself. "He wouldn't say he would and then back out. He couldn't be that cruel!"

But it was an assurance lacking entire confidence. Based upon her recent contact with Gary Elliott, his telephoned proposal seemed bona fide, believable. Yet, when she remembered the Gary Elliott whose career Matt Landerson had looked upon with such disdain, such a proposal seemed unreal and out of character. It was a career concerning which Starr's personal knowledge was limited. Gary Elliott, at the age of fifteen years, had been sent away to school and, since that time, had spent as little of his time as possible upon the Broken Bar. But she remembered vividly her father's estimate of him.

"I never liked old T. J. Elliott on account of the way he treated that first wife of his, as well as for personal reasons. But he was a man, in spite of his faults. But that son of his—! He's a softy and a sneak, that kid! Schoolin' went to his head, all right; but not the way it should've done. He's no-account. And, from the tales I've heard, that's not the worst of it."

Softy, sneak. Starr tried to fit those words to the man with whom she had been associated these past ten days. Matt Landerson had seldom been mistaken in his judgment of men, she knew; and he would never have damned a man so heartily unless he had been very sure. In fact, the few brief contacts Starr had had with Gary as a boy had justified her father's estimate of him. But now . . .

Her mind ran down the list of the surprises

she had found in him these past ten days. His gentleness; his slow, clean smile; his steady eyes, the passionate intensity of his swift admiration for The Star. This last was close to a miracle, she thought, for Gary Elliott had never shown the slightest love for land. And he had gauged the value and the possibilities of The Star with the eye of an expert.

Last, and even more remarkable, had come this offer for the purchase of The Notch.

These things all added up to such and such a sum. The total startled her and she went back over the addition in her mind. But she nodded finally, and smiled, and filed the answer in her mind.

She thought, irrelevantly, "If he builds a dam in The Notch, I'll have to grade the old wet-weather road around the rim."

They came down finally into the outskirts of the town and Starr turned guiltily to glance at the prim, upright little lady at her side. Mrs. McElvey had flatly refused to permit this evening visit to the Broken Bar unless Starr were provided with an escort for the homeward trip.

"It's bad enough, your spendin' all this time with Gary Elliott at best. Your father never would approve of it, and I most certainly do not! But when it means drivin' all that way back home at night alone, that's where my foot comes down! I'm going! As far as Coronado, anyway. I'll drop in on Aggie Donahue. Or if she ain't home, I'll see a moving picture show. And you be back in Coronado by dark, young lady! Mind, now! Fine thing 'twould be indeed —a scandal—you and Gary Elliott!"

Starr smiled as she remembered the old lady's disdainful sniff. She said, "I haven't been very good company, have I, Mother Mac? I'm so excited over all this. . . ."

"Excited? Pooh! What's Gary Elliott to get excited at?"

"Not at Gary, silly! About selling The Notch. It would be pretty fine, wouldn't it, if we could build The Star back up again? And we can, too, if Gary buys that land."

"I wouldn't count on it," Mrs. McElvey said sparingly. "I ain't never seen good fruit off a bad tree yet, and don't expect to see it now. There's somethin' back of it. You'll see!"

And when Starr stopped the car before the Donahue gate and reached across to open the door, Mrs. McElvey clutched at her arm. "Please, honey, don't you go! There's somethin' wicked back of this! He'll never buy that land, child; never in this world! It's like Tom said: he hates the land. It just ain't natural. It worries me, the way he's makin' up to you."

"But I promised, Mother Mac. I've got to go. I *want* to go! This is our only chance. I couldn't turn it down. . . . Don't worry now. I'll be all right."

She stopped in Coronado to talk for a moment with Dr. Northup and then drove out along the glaring pavement toward the Broken Bar. Midway from town, she passed a rider on an ambling, dusty black and, when he turned to stare at her, she thought she saw a glint of recognition in his eyes. She felt, as well, that she had seen the man somewhere before; and yet she knew that he was a stranger here. The vague familiarity puzzled her.

But she had forgotten all that before she reached the Broken Bar. Lary came down the broad steps from the porch as she swung in beside the house and she faced him soberly, making no move as yet to leave the car.

"Just to make sure that I'm not here under a misapprehension," she said, "would you mind repeating that proposition you made over the telephone?"

He grinned. "One hundred and six thousand dollars for all land under your ownership south of a line drawn east and west along the top of the approximately two-mile-long grade north of The Notch. Five thousand down as binder for a sixty-day option to be signed by you; said five thousand to apply against the purchase price, if, as and when."

Her smile was one of quick relief. "So businesslike!" she murmured. "If, as and when what?"

"Paid!" Day said. "Don't tell me you're boostin' the price?"

She shook her head. "The price is—generous. And it's a deal, Gary." She held out her hand to seal the bargain and Day took it gravely, thinking how straight-forward, man-to-man she was, and yet how feminine.

"It's a deal," he said. "I've drawn up the option for your signature. Here it is. And here's the check. . . . And here's a pen! Sign on the dotted line!"

She read the slip of paper he presented her; glanced at the check. He wondered if she were familiar with Gary Elliott's signature; remembered that she could not be. Still, the signature on the check was by no means a discreditable forgery. Gary Elliott's rough scrawl was not too difficult to imitate and Day had practiced it with care. And any small dissimilarities could be explained, he knew, with Northup's help.

But Starr found no fault with it. She signed the option after reading it and sighed. "That's a relief!" she said. "Of course, I was pretty sure you meant what you said, and that you said what I thought you said; but I'm not used to having dreams come true and, as the hours went by, I began to doubt."

"Then why didn't you come sooner, to make sure?"

She laughed. "After all, I've been an almost daily visitor here these past ten days. I could hardly admit that I couldn't wait until the appointed time, could I? And, anyway, how was I to know you hadn't had enough of me?"

"Did my invitation sound like I'd had enough of you?"

"It sounded like a threat! Fear brought me here!"

She stepped down then and took his arm, laughing as she fell into step with him. They walked together to the broad verandah where Chang had placed two easy chairs. Starr sank into one of them and, as Day stood over her, she tipped her head far back to frown at him.

"It's all so unlike you, Gary," she said. "Unlike the Gary Elliott you were, or that I thought you were."

Her pause did not prepare him for the question that came after it. "You *are* Gary Elliott, aren't you? . . . Or—are you?"

She said it jokingly, but still it startled him. He laughed a little, but it seemed to him that his laughter sounded forced. He turned to draw the second chair up nearer hers, glad of the momentary break the movement gave in which to set his face in readiness to meet her scrutiny.

He said, "That's what they tell me, anyway. I couldn't swear to it."

And suddenly he found himself despising the implied untruth that statement held. Until now, the thing had seemed a game; a game with serious aspects offset by a worthwhile reward. But now it was a game that he disliked. Under Starr Landerson's clear, friendly gaze, his masquerade seemed somehow cheap. He wished that he could shuck it off. He thought, "Why not? Why not tell her the truth?"

But she was smiling when he dared to look at her; smiling and nodding her acceptance of his lie. The moment for confession had slipped past.

"That memory of yours!" she said. "It must be convenient, Gary, forgetting all the past; starting with a clean new sheet."

"It's awkward, too," he said deliberately. "I had two callers this morning. Luckily Doc Northup was here to introduce 'em." He glanced at her. "Brett Randall and Lem Marsden came over to talk to me about this deal of ours."

Chang came between them then, all smiles and bows as he set up the table for their meal. But Starr was seemingly oblivious of him.

"How did they know about it? What did they say?"

Day shrugged. "Seems Randall's got a girl friend in the telephone office. That's worth knowin', by the way . . . They didn't seem to like our little deal."

He leaned toward her suddenly. "Just why does Randall want that particular piece of land?"

"I didn't know he did." Starr's eyes showed plain bewilderment. "I knew he wanted Star Valley, of course."

Day shook his head. "It's the south end of it

that interests Randall particularly. And here's the funny part. It seems that Randall and—" He almost said, "And Gary Elliott." He caught himself in time and went on more carefully. "It seems that Randall and I are supposed to be in cahoots on some deal involvin' that same land. That is, I'm supposed to know why Randall wants it. In fact, he thinks I do know why; that I'm fakin' this amnesia business just to double-cross him. He's real indignant about it."

Chang served them deftly, moving silently on slippered feet. Starr sat in silence till the man had gone. Once Lary thought he saw a gleam of sly amusement in her eyes. But she was thoughtful when she spoke at last.

"But you're going through with it." It was hardly a question; more, Day thought, judged by its tone, a compliment. That puzzled him.

"Of course I'm going through with it."

She smiled at him. "Then let's forget it, shall we? ... What about the other part of your proposition?"

"Grazing privileges in Star Valley?" Day leaned forward eagerly. "Just this: My range is shot. Vale tells me there isn't grass enough for the cattle on it already, to say nothing of the stuff I've just—acquired." He flushed a little, but went on. "So I thought if I could shove my stuff on your range, payin' you for grazin' rights, of course, we'd both be benefited. You see, I've got a hunch that beef is goin' up. This drought has forced a lot of cattlemen to unload and that's pushed the market down; but most of that unloadin's over now. And because of it, there's bound to be a shortage of beef. Seems to me the market ought to climb. I figure in sixty days I'll make enough, what with a better market plus the pounds my cattle will put on once they get proper feed, to take up that option and have some pocket money left. And you'll be makin' somethin' out of it at the same time."

The mealtime passed in pleasant talk, marked here and there with friendly silences. And in both talk and silence Lary found a close communion with this girl that filled him with a keen delight; a communion different from her attitude toward him before. Starr's mind was quick and with a masculine directness that appealed to him. There was no coquetry in her, he thought, nor any sham.

An hour passed before Chang took away the table and held lighted matches for their cigarettes. The sun was sinking to the fiery crater that awaited it behind the western hills and, in the ruddy sunset light, the scene before them lost its harsh, parched ugliness; became transformed and beautiful. Long shadows stretching far across the Coronado range deepened from blue-grey to purple and gave way to rosy highlights where the sun still touched. The corrals and barns below the house sank into darkness while an afterglow still washed the upper yard and once Starr moved a little nervously and said, "There's someone there."

Day straightened. "Where?"

But when she pointed out the place to him, down where the mesa rim dropped steeply to the barns, there was no movement there and Day sat back again. "A bird," he said, "or some stray dog." And turned to watch once more the play of lights upon her hair.

Her nearness filled him with a strange, sweet peace. He spoke at last, quite softy. "I've just remembered something, Starr," he said. "A kiss . . . the night I went away to school."

It was an insane thing to say, he knew; a mad, foolhardy risk. And, more than that, it was a new, unnecessary lie. Almost before the words were out, he wished that he could snatch them back. But they were gone and, paradoxically, Day knew that he was glad. What would Starr say?

13

SHE turned a startled glance to him. A moment passed before she spoke and, when she did, her voice was low and filled with mellow cadences. "It's strange—that you should suddenly remember—that," she said.

"It's stranger still that I should ever have forgotten it!"

He leaned toward her suddenly and took her hand. A rifle shot lashed viciously across the yard and a hot wind touched fleetingly across the nape of Lary's neck. Out of the corner of his eyes, he caught a glimpse of licking flame that cut the shadow at the mesa's rim and then was gone. He heard Starr's quick intake of breath. He caught her in his arms and lifted her; wheeled swiftly toward the door. A second bullet smashed into the wall. Day heard his own voice framing bitter, prayerful oaths. The door stood open and he lunged inside; stepped to the left into the shelter of the wall.

Starr clung to him, her body weightless in his arms. He said, "Are you all right?"

"All right. And you?"

He said, "That fool! He might've killed you!"

She laughed, shakily. "It wasn't me he meant to kill!"

For one long moment he stood motionless, still holding her, the fragrance of her hair sweet in his nostrils like a rare perfume. He said, "I love you, Starr! I haven't any right to tell you that. But it's the truth."

A yell, shrill, high and challenging, went rocketing across the night and something in the sound of it struck recognition in Day's mind. "Pop Greer!" A horse's hoofs beat out a swift tattoo across the yard. Day put Starr down and reached above her head to where a rifle hung on wooden pegs above the door. He jerked the bolt and saw a cartridge slide into the breech. He plunged outside.

A horseman swerved across his vision at a headlong run and, even in that fading light, Day instantly identified Pop Greer. Day cleared the porch in three long strides. A zig-zag trail ran down beyond the mesa's rim toward the barns and Greer spurred into it.

Ahead of Greer, a shadow fled and turned at bay. Day heard Greer's heavy gun speak once and, following that, the whip-like crack of a third rifle shot. He flung his own gun up to aim but, as he moved, the shadow flitted into nothingness. Greer fired again.

Day lunged at the descent but missed the trail and stumbled crashing through thick underbrush. He heard Greer's horse plow gravel in a sliding halt. Somewhere ahead, men's voices rose in a hoarse tangle of unintelligible sound. Day smashed through a barrier of thorny brush to reach the lower yard.

A black horse stood with lowered head beside the barn and, under him, a small still figure sprawled upon the ground. The horse shied nervously as Day dropped to his knees beside Pop Greer.

"Pop! How bad you hit?" His voice was harsh, unnatural.

Greer said, "You take it easy, son. Don't try —to pick me up. I'm shot—in two. At that— I'll bet a man a hat I put my mark on *him!*"

Day said, "You'll be all right. You've got to be! I'll get a doctor here. . . ."

But Greer's thin fingers clutched his arm. "Don't leave me, son. . . . And let me do—the talkin'. I ain't—got long."

Greer coughed and the sound of it tore something in Lary's heart. The fingers tightened on his arm.

"I was—back o' the house—waitin' for your company t' leave—when I heard the first shot. I had t'—talk to you. I met a man I knew—in town today. A minin' man. Name of Calahan. Seems Calahan is runnin' down a rumor—that somebody's struck pay dirt—near here. Wanted me t' do some prospectin'. I told him I would. Figured it was a—chance—for me to stick around—sort of in the background like—in case you needed me."

Greer smiled. His voice was weaker now. "I won't be doin' any more—prospectin', I reckon. But—I'm glad I came!"

He rallied momentarily. "What for they want to kill you, son? You know?"

Day shook his head. "I'm buyin' some land some other people want," he said huskily. "That might be back of it."

Greer nodded thoughtfully. "And some cows. Star cattle, wasn't it? Foreclosed on 'em. . . . I heard—somethin' like that. . . . And that reminds me—of another thing. What would Star-branded cows—be doin'—in the hills?"

Day thought Greer's mind was wandering. "I wouldn't know, Pop," he said gently.

"Find out!" Greer's voice whipped back at him with something of its old vitality. "I seen 'em—on my way in here." The effort made him cough again. His voice lost force and Day bent close to catch his words. "You're—on the right track, son. About—that other thing. Go through with it. But—watch your step! You've —stumbled onto somethin'—big. Don't let 'em —dry-gulch you."

Somewhere, far off, a motor sputtered as it came to life; caught suddenly and swelled to a full-throated roar. The sound changed to a whine as gears came into mesh. A car gained speed and drew away.

Greer's hand slid down along Day's arm. "You've been a damn good son to me," Greer said. "So long. Be . . . seein' you."

Pop Greer was dead.

Day sat for some time, motionless, numbed by the shock of it. His eyes burned hotly with an unsatisfied desire for tears. Grief, anger and remorse took turns with him; fused swiftly to a white-hot hate. His fingers tightened on the rifle he still held; clenched on the steel until it bruised his flesh. "I'll even this, so help me God!" The oath was comforting.

The sound of heels click-clacking on the trail

above him penetrated to Day's consciousness. That would be Starr. Still other heavier footfalls came toward him from beyond the barn. A man ran into view as Day stood up; a man with a lantern swinging loosely in one hand, a rifle slung across the other arm. It was Red Vale. He halted, facing Day. Behind him, other men appeared: Joe Travis, Tommy Ladd and Buck Dupree. These were the riders for the Broken Bar. They stood in silence, gazing down at Greer.

Day said, "Who's been here, Vale? Who fired those shots?"

Vale shook his head. "Don't know," he said. "We was all in the bunkhouse, playin' cards, when the first shot came. Thought it was a car backfirin', at first."

Joe Travis said, "I heard a car, right afterward. I reckon that was him, hightailin' it."

Starr Landerson touched Lary's arm. "I tried to phone the Sheriff, Gary," she said. "The phone was dead."

Day stooped and lifted Greer's limp body in his arms. Starr took the lantern from Red Vale and led the way. Day followed her and Vale came after him; then Travis and Dupree and Tommy Ladd. They made a weird procession as they climbed the cliff; five living men, a dead man and a girl, like votaries in some strange ritual. And, last in line, Greer's tall black horse walked mincingly with lowered head, unburdened now.

Day laid Greer's body on a bed in the big house and stood beside it for a moment, looking down at it. Death shrinks a man, somehow, and Greer, not large in life, seemed smaller still in death. But he lay calm and peacefully, as if asleep.

"So long," Day whispered brokenly. "*Vaya con Dios*, Pop." He turned and tiptoed from the room. Starr faced him as he closed the door. Outside, he heard the husky murmur of voices where Red Vale and the other men awaited him. Somewhere, deep in the house, a clock struck eight vibrating strokes. The sound sent shivers down Day's spine. He leaned back, sick and spent, against the wall. Starr crossed the room to stand beside him and he reached out blindly and took both her hands.

The contact steadied him. He straightened and stood looking down at her. He spoke at last, his dull voice matching the bleak misery that glazed his eyes.

"You say the phone is dead?"

She nodded.

"Then I'll have to go to town with you. I'll have to notify the coroner and get the law started—"

He broke off abruptly, eyes narrowing, jaw clenched until the muscles at its base stood out in throbbing lumps. The law, eh? Lem Marsden! The name stood out in vivid lettering against his brain. He smiled, and something in that smile made Starr draw back from him.

"Let's go!" he said.

A sudden silence fell upon the little group that surrounded the lantern on the front porch as Starr and Day came out to them, but Day walked past them and on down the steps without a word. Starr paused briefly and exchanged a word or two with Vale, then followed Lary to the car. The black horse moved away as she approached and Day turned to face her. She saw, with an odd sense of unreality, that he was armed. A holstered gun swung low against his leg, suspended from a sagging cartridge belt, and even as he turned to her he stooped and tied the holster-thong above his knee.

He straightened then and held the door for her. "I might need this," he said with strange embarrassment. "It's—his. He dropped the gun he was usin', I reckon, when he was hit. But I found this other one in his saddle bags."

She might have spoken, but a memory halted her; a memory of Matt Landerson when he, too, years ago, had strapped a gun upon his leg and gone to town. Starr barely could remember it. She did not know—had never known—what that old quarrel had been; but she remembered vividly how he had bade his wife, and Starr, goodbye. In just this casual, half-apologetic tone. And Landerson had killed a man that day . . . Her fingers on the steering wheel felt cold.

Day did not speak again until their journey was half done. He sat beside her, his long legs doubled up so that his knees could rest against the instrument panel, his body swaying lightly to the movement of the car, his eyes half closed. A dozen times she glanced at him and would have spoken, but each time the look of him discouraged her. His face was grim and set and yet she sensed an eagerness in him, a latent force that somehow frightened her. Seen in the half-light from the small bulb in the instrument panel of the car, his face seemed angular and strongly carved. He seemed entirely unaware of her, so lost in thought that when he spoke at last it startled her.

"That option, Starr—we can't go through with that. I was a fool."

The meaning of his words avoided her until his voice had ceased. It left her numb. She thought, "So Mother Mac was right! He's backing out! . . . But why? Why did he let me think—?" She dared not look at him. Her voice was dull and toneless when she answered him.

"All right. Just as you say."

She felt his movement; knew that he had turned to look at her. He must have sensed her thought, because he said, "Aw, Starr, don't get me wrong! I didn't mean the deal was off. I meant, we'll have to handle it a different way, that's all."

The swift reaction left her trembling. A moment passed before she dared to trust her voice. She said, "What do you mean?"

"Just this. When we get to town, we'll find Doc Northup and get him to help us draw up papers to complete the deal right now. I said I'd give you a hundred and six thousand for the land. All right. Randall said today that those cattle I took from you by foreclosure were worth ninety-odd thousand at the market. Call it ninety-one thousand. I'll give you a bill of sale for those cattle, plus my check for fifteen thousand, in return for a quit-claim deed on your land south of the top of that slope above The Notch. The only difference between this and the option idea is that this way the deal'll be closed and you'll be takin' the chance of any rise or fall in the beef market instead of me takin' it. Is it a deal?"

"Of course. But why?"

He shrugged. "Let's not go into that."

"Oh, yes, we will go into it! Why have you changed your mind so suddenly?"

"Well.... Somebody took a shot at me tonight; somebody who didn't want this deal of ours to go through. If he'd got me, that option thing would have lapsed and all you'd've had to show for it would've been my check for five thousand dollars. And five thousand dollars wouldn't've been worth a damn to you when it came to savin' your ranch."

She nodded. "And—you think they'll try again!"

"I hope they do! Next time—"

She saw his fingers crook and clench until the knuckles stood out white. She dropped her hand upon his rigid fist. "I suppose it's no use asking you to—go away, Gary? Just for a little while, until this blows over?"

He shook his head. "Not now. Not after this, tonight."

She said, "You'd win, that way. You'd get the land; I save The Star . . . and you'd be safe."

"And the man who killed Pop Greer would go scot-free!"

The name slipped out of him. He shot a startled look at Starr. She was pulling the car to one side now, slowing to a halt before the Northup house. Apparently the slip had gone unnoticed. Perhaps the name meant nothing to her. He breathed a grateful oath as he got out and walked around the car to hand Starr down. He took her arm to guide her up the steps to Northup's door, but Starr held back. He turned. She stood quite close to him, her head tipped back so that the light from Northup's window lent a mellow radiance to her face. Her words bewildered him.

"I'm grateful, Gary. I understand—a lot of things—tonight. Things that puzzled me before. And, even if this deal of ours should—fail—I'll still be grateful. You'll remember that, won't you?"

He said, "But it can't fail, can it?... Anyway, this isn't charity. I'm really driving a hard bargain. That dam will be worth a dozen times...."

But he was thinking. "What does she understand?" The thought befuddled him. He stumbled and his voice trailed off. Northup's door opened before he could find words again.

"That you, Starr?... Hello! I see it is! Properly escorted, too. I was just startin' out to see if you'd had car trouble or anything. Mrs. Mac phoned me a while ago. Said she'd tried to call you at the Broken Bar and couldn't get through. She was upset. Come in. I'll call her now. Tell her you're here."

He was at the telephone when they entered and they waited, listening to his reassurances to Mother Mac. He was chuckling as he hung the receiver on its hook again. "Like an old hen with one chick, that woman!" he growled. "Wouldn't take my word for anything! She's comin' over here to see for herself! Like as not she'll give you a piece of her mind, Gary, for keepin' Starr out so late!... Sit down, you two. What's wrong with your telephone, young man? It worked all right the last time I called you."

Day said, "The wire's been cut."

Northup grunted and flung up his head. "Wires cut?" He glanced at Starr, then back to Day again. "Trouble, eh?... All right; out with it!"

Day told him in a dozen clipped, curt sentences. A knock sounded on the outer door as his voice ceased and Northup opened it. Mrs. McElvey bustled in, clucking busily as her delight at seeing Starr waged war with her tart comments aimed at Elliott. But Northup silenced her.

"Hush, Mother Mac! Starr's here, and safe. We've other fish to fry. A man's been killed."

He turned to Day. "The dead man is—Pop, eh? The man who came to see me this mornin'?"

Lary nodded.

"Who killed him?" Northup's voice lashed out with sudden force.

"I don't know."

"But you've got an opinion! Out with it, boy!"

"Well.... It would have to be somebody opposed to this deal of mine with—Miss Landerson, wouldn't it? Who else would gain by killin' me? . . . And the only ones I know opposed to that are—Randall and Marsden."

Northup grunted. "I figured that was how your mind was runnin'," he said. "What'd you say if I was to tell you that Brett Randall is right now presidin' at a lodge meeting in the Elks Hall, and has been there to my personal knowledge since six o'clock? I know, because the shindig started out as a banquet and I was there. . . . And Lem Marsden bought a ticket for San Francisco this evenin' and took the train at 6:55 with a delegation from the aforementioned banquet to see him off."

Day shrugged. "I'd say that those alibis were good; almost too good! And, anyway, it's always possible for a man to hire another man to do his dirty work."

Northup nodded. "Smart boy! I just didn't want you wastin' your time on any false ideas, that's all."

Day told him then of his plan for altering the deal with Starr. The plan won Northup's hearty approval and he drew the necessary papers in his own crisp hand, adding his own signature as witness together with that of Mother Mac.

Later, Northup drove with Day back to the Broken Bar after having notified a deputy left in charge by Marsden during his absence. "He'll be out in the morning," Northup explained. "Claims there's nothin' he could do tonight, and I reckon he's right."

Day nodded. But his thoughts were busy with Starr's puzzling remark. "I understand—a lot of things—tonight. Things that puzzled me before." What did it mean? Had she seen through his masquerade? He thought that she had not. Surely she made no sign of noticing his use of Pop Greer's name.

It struck him finally that she referred to his avowal of his love for her. His proffered help in the matter of the land had puzzled her; was now explained. That must be it.

And so his thoughts turned, satisfied, to other things.

He would have been less confident, perhaps, had he but known of Starr's remark that night to Mother Mac. Mrs. McElvey's opinion of Gary Elliott had suffered a severe shock tonight, for not even she could overlook the value of tonight's transaction to Starr Landerson. But she was slow to yield.

"I'd trot right back to town first thing in the mornin', if I was you, and cash that check!" she said. "Be like the man to change his mind!

He ain't himself, you know. Like as not if he got his memory back, he'd stop payment on it."

Starr did not answer for a time and the old lady turned to stare at her. Starr's lips were curved in a secretive smile.

"No, Mother Mac," she said. "I won't do that. In fact, I don't intend to cash that check at all! Not now, at least. Not till we see how things—turn out!"

14

"YOU say you was settin' on the porch, here, and somebody fired at you. Any witness t' that?"

Haines, the deputy left in charge during Marsden's absence, was handling the inquiry into Pop Greer's death. It was the morning following the murder and Haines had brought two men with him besides the coroner. Dr. Jason Northup, truant from his duties for the moment, had made the introductions.

"One," Day said. "Miss Landerson."

Haines shot a startled glance at him, but Lary made no comment. Evidently the news of the new and friendlier relations between the Star and the Broken Bar had not yet reached the sheriff's underlings.

"You got any idea where the shot came from?"

"I saw the flash the first time he fired. I'll show you."

Day led the way across the yard. Northup and Haines walked beside him and the others followed curiously. They halted where the mesa dropped off sharply into buckbrush that clung precariously against the rocky slope and Day pointed.

"It was about here, I think. No, to the right a yard. There's where he knelt."

A shallow shelf of yellow soil lay, bare of brush, a yard below the mesa rim and there, indelibly marked, the story of the ambush was told in characters not hard to read. A man's right boot had left its imprint there and, back of that, the cup-shaped dent left by a knee was visible.

Haines grunted, "Knelt t' fire, eh? Reckon by kneelin' that-a-way he got a solid rest against the bank."

He stooped and would have clambered down, but Lary caught his arm. "I wouldn't mess around down there, if I were you. You'll want a cast of that boot track."

Haines scowled at him. "I'm runnin' this, young feller!" he said irritably. "How'm I gonna take a cast, I'd like t' know? And what's the use? The track ain't plain enough t' do us any good. Feller must've moved his foot, the way the track is blurred."

Northup glanced at Day. "Might as well be

thorough, though, eh, Haines? I've got some plaster-Paris in my car. Be a feather in your cap, eh, if you could land this hombre before Marsden gets back? That track might be just the evidence you need. Seems to be about the *only* evidence."

Haines cleared his throat. "That's a fact," he said. "Well, Doc, you fetch the stuff. We'll make a cast, just in case."

He turned to Day again. "Well, Elliott? What happened next?"

"Two shots from here; I told you that, didn't I? I reckon you'll find the empty cartridges down there somewhere. . . . When he fired the second time, I was hustlin' Miss Landerson into the house. About a minute later I heard a horse runnin', and someone yelled. I grabbed a rifle and came outside. I saw Pop—Brown, the man who was killed, ridin' across the yard. I ran down this way. Pop hit the path yonder and I saw a man ahead of him turn and fire at him. Pop fired twice. I tried to get a bead on the man myself but he ducked out of sight into the brush. When I got down the hill, Pop was on the ground yonder by the barn."

"What was he doin' here, anyway? Stranger, wasn't he?"

"He was a friend of mine. He told me before he died that he rode up just a few minutes before the shootin', saw I had company and was sort of hesitatin', wonderin' whether to butt in or not, when that first shot was fired. It took him a minute or so to get his gun out of his saddle bags."

Northup returned as Lary finished speaking, and Chang came after him with a bucket of water. "I'll make the cast, Haines, if you like," Northup suggested. "I'm used to handlin' this stuff."

Haines nodded and led the way down the narrow path toward the barns. Midway, Day stooped and picked a gun from underneath a bush. Haines snatched it angrily.

"What's that?"

"I reckon it's the gun Pop was usin'," Day suggested. "He likely dropped it when he was hit."

Haines grunted and turned the weapon in his hand. "Looks like you're right," he admitted. "Two empty shells in it, anyway; and you said the old man fired two shots. Too bad he wasn't a better shot. Saved us a heap o' trouble if he'd grooved that hombre, eh?"

Day said, "You won't find many better shots

with a six gun than Pop was, I reckon. But this was at a runnin' target, in the dark, off a horse buck-jumpin' down a right steep grade."

He broke off suddenly, remembering. Pop Greer had said, "At that, I'll bet a man a hat I put my mark on him!" And there was blood here on the path. But that might be Greer's blood, spilled as the black horse carried him on down the slope or later, when they bore his body to the house. It was true, Day knew that Greer—like many experts with a gun—could sometimes tell, apparently by some sixth sense, when he had made a scoring shot. But this was different. "He might've had his gun on the target," Day thought, "but even then he might've missed. The man was movin' fast . . . I'll just tell Northup to look out for any gunshot wounds, in case. That ought to cover it."

Red Vale came past the corner of the barn as they approached and Lary paused to speak to him. "We'll move those Star cattle back onto Star range, Vale," he said. "You might as well get at it."

He saw the blank astonishment on Vale's dour face, but the man made no remark. Day turned to follow Haines, but paused. "On second thought," he said, "suppose you saddle a horse for me. I'll ride along with you."

It would be easier, he thought, if he had work to occupy his mind. But Haines was staring at him when he turned. "Not sellin' them cattle, eh?"

Day shook his head. "The market can't get worse," he said. "The way I figure it, it's due to rise.... You need me here?"

Haines grunted an unwilling negative. Day glanced up the hill. Northup and the other two deputies were busy over the tracks on the outcropping ledge. "I'd better go up and say goodbye to Northup," Day thought.

Red Vale was grinning as he passed Day's orders to his men. "We're movin' the Landerson stuff back into the Valley," he said. "Which is a break for us, eh, boys? And here's a treat: The boss is ridin' with us underlings today!"

Buck Dupree spat accurately at an industrious tumble-bug. "H'mm! Givin' us another crack at them cows, is he? Nice o' him, by God it is!... Hey, Red! You was wishin' the other day you could be real sure about the boss' memory, wasn't you? If he was fakin' it or not. Well, here's your chance! Saddle Saint for him.

If he gets on The Saint, you'll know he's lost his memory for sure. If he's in his right mind, all hell couldn't persuade him t' do it. And, if he makes a fuss. . . . Well, it was all a joke."

There was a silence while the four men savoured the full flavor of the joke. Vale laughed. "Buck, you're a card! Come on!"

He snatched a saddle from the corral fence. A slant-hipped, sleepy-eyed grey gelding side-stepped warily as Vale approached but made no actual effort to escape. The Saint was wise. He knew from bitter memory that there was no escape from man; that flight would merely earn a snaring rope to his heels and bruise his ribs. He closed his eyes as Vale cinched the saddle on him. Not even the unexpected indignity of a bit in his mouth was worth protesting. The bridle puzzled him a little, though. Usually they left the bridle off. Few men who have mounted The Saint had needed reins. Not, certainly, for very long.

Vale glanced up warily as Day appeared. The other men were saddling and Lary lit a cigarette. Vale took a long, deep breath. "Maybe you better fork him here in the corral, boss," Vale said tentatively. "It's been a while since he was rode. He might come untwisted on you."

Day shrugged and stepped through the corral gate. The grey looked half asleep, he thought. Still, if he had been corralled and fed since Elliott rode him last . . .

He took the reins. The grey cocked one ear back at him. Joe Travis, back of Day and outside the corral, clutched Red Vale's arm. "He's gonna do it!" Vale nodded. Day caught the saddle horn and swung aloft. The grey horse shuddered as his head went down.

"Look out!" Dupree's hoarse shout broke irresistibly. He had not meant to speak. "Look out! He's gonna come apart!"

Vale's lip curled back across his teeth. The grey horse lunged, uncoiling like a mighty spring. He shot aloft, swift forefeet striking at the air, so that he seemed to climb. He grunted with the effort of that leap and Red Vale grunted too, knowing the back-snapping force of it.

That first lunge smashed the saddle horn into Day's groin. He gasped and swore. The grey came down, side-slipping with pile-driving force. A muscle in Day's neck popped audibly. The grey spun dizzily, his head thrust back, teeth gleaming as he reached for Lary's foot.

Day used the six-foot reins, quirtlike, to lash the horse across the ears. Another lunge.

Instinctively, Day rode. Instinctively, he knew that this was no mere saddle horse working off the pent-up dynamite of grain and laziness. But it was work; hard, savage work that gave his mental teeth a thing to bite down on. Here, momentarily at least, he could forget the tangled web of vague cross-purposes that had entangled him; forget Pop Greer. He let his voice rip free in one long yell. He found the cadence of the grey's insanity. The horse sun-fished and squealed. Dust fogged around them in an acrid cloud.

Vale's lips came down across his teeth again. His grin was gone. "By God!" he gasped. "By God, he's *ridin'* him!"

"I'd tell a man!" Joe Travis said. "He's forgot a-plenty, all right, or he never would've forked The Saint! But he sure ain't forgot how t' ride!"

"*He never knew!*" Vale said. "Not how to ride like that!"

"He knows it now, all right! Look at him scratch that horse!"

The grey swapped ends. The vicious force of it sent fiery pain along Day's thighs. His nose was bleeding now and the salt taste of blood was in his mouth. He wondered how a little horse could fight so hard so long. The sheer explosive force of that first lunge was in the tenth—the twentieth—as well. And this had lasted twice as long as any Rodeo ride. Once, as they cleared the dust, Day caught a glimpse of Northup watching him. That proved the time. How long had it taken Northup to come down the hill, around the barn? Too long. Day's brain felt numb.

The horse lunged forward suddenly toward the fence. It was a zig-zag, crazy course, each jump a smashing, muscle-wrenching blow. But there was purpose in it. The horse was weakening. Why not? Day's knees were slipping, too. He thought, "He's figurin' to smash my leg against the fence."

The horse wheeled suddenly and flung his weight toward the barrier. "*Look out!*" The doctor's hoarse, fear-ridden shout came through the fog to Lary's consciousness. He thought, "I'm lookin' out the best I can!"

He gripped the saddle horn with both hands as the grey horse turned; leaned forward, flinging both legs up and out. He cleared the fence in one long vault; heard the grey smash into it. He fell and rolled. When he sat up, a man was bending over him.

"I'm all right, Doc."

Past Northup's legs he glimpsed Vale's face. Vale's grin was mocking, truculent. It struck the spark. The dull resentment that had smouldered in Day's heart for weeks leaped into flame. Hurt after hurt had added fuel to feed a slumbering fire in him: arrest, the trial, imprisonment, Greer's death. Here was an outlet for that wrath. He lurched erect; stood swaying on a drunken world. Northup would have steadied him but Day struck Northup's hand aside.

"You saddled that horse for me, Vale." His voice was low, but there was a purring undertone in it. The last word snapped. "Why?"

Vale shrugged. "Why not?" he said. "We thought The Saint might give you back your—memory!"

The ground stopped pitching and Day moved ahead a pace or two. A yard from Vale he halted and stood balanced on his toes. The grin on Vale's face dissolved. Day said, "Just what's the meanin' back of that?"

Vale frowned; drew back a step. "Don't crowd me, mister!" he said, very low. "You can't bluff me, you know! I know too much!"

"Such as?"

"You asked for it!" Vale said. "Look, Haines! This guy ain't—"

Day rocked ahead, his left fist hooking up in a swift arc. It was unethical, perhaps. Red Vale was armed and so was Day. Vale, used to guns, had watched Day's poised right hand. That hand had jerked and darted down. Vale's gun was half outside its sheath when Day's left fist crashed home.

Vale's head snapped back. His body sagged and seemed to telescope. Knee, hip and shoulder struck in a limp fall. Day stooped and took the half-drawn gun; tossed it to Haines. Vale groaned and twisted and sat up.

"You're fired!" Day said. He glanced at the tight group by the corral; Joe Travis, Tommy Ladd and Buck Dupree. "That goes for you three, too . . . Well, Vale? You want to talk?"

Vale staggered up. Instinctively, his hand slid up inquiringly until it touched the empty holster on his hip. He shrugged. "Not now," he said. "Later!"

Day nodded. "Any time!" he said.

Vale rubbed his jaw. "You'll hear from me, all right! Don't think you won't!"

Day turned and walked past Northup, past

the corner of the barn, and up the steep incline toward the house. He heard Northup's heavy footsteps following him. The knowledge that the doctor's burly body shielded him was comforting. He reached the house and passed inside; sat down. But Northup halted in the door.

Day said, "You know where I can hire me some good cowhands?"

Northup chuckled quietly. "You won't be needin' em!" he said. "Son, Gary Elliott could never ride like that!"

"I know," Day shrugged. "I should've let that sleepy lookin' devil pile me, I reckon. I didn't think of it in time. Vale's wise to me."

"Not only wise, but sore! ever notice how insulted a gunman gets when somebody hangs a swingin' punch along his jaw?" The big man's laughter rumbled through the room. "Insults 'em mightily, that does! Proves that folks lack the proper respect for their reputation as bad men!"

"You think he'll talk?"

"I ain't just sure. I was surprised when he didn't blurt it out right after you hit him. Since he didn't do that, I'm wondering. He may be figurin' to play a waiting game. He may have an axe to grind somewhere."

Day nodded thoughtfully. "I reckon the smart thing for me to do would be to run. But —I can't do that. Not with Greer layin' dead in there . . . Then, too, I've got to get those cattle back to Starr. Possession is nine points of the law, they say. If anything happens to me, I want her to have those nine points."

He stood up restlessly and paced the floor. "Another thing. Just before Greer died, he said that he was sure he scored a hit. He might've been wrong, of course. But I wanted you to know. You just bear it in mind, in case somebody shows up with a suspicious gunshot wound."

Northup nodded. "And, in the meantime, what'll you be doin', son?"

"First, I aim to hire a crew and move those cows. After that—" He shrugged. "I aim to get the man who killed Pop Greer. I don't know how, but—there it is."

Northup frowned. "You'd better leave that to the law, hadn't you?" He raised one hand placatingly in answer to Lary's angry protest. "I know! You're thinkin' that the law—Lem

Marsden, anyway—won't be much help. But just the same—"

Day interrupted him. "Did you finish makin' the cast of that track?"

"Yes. And we found a couple of ejected cartridges, too. Thirty-thirties, Winchester. A lot of good they'll do! There ain't more than a thousand rifles like that in this county, I reckon. And the boot track was so smeared it don't amount to shucks as far as provin' anything's concerned."

A horse's hoofs rang sharply in the lower yard. Day turned to the window. The single hoofbeats became four and Lary caught a glimpse of Vale and his three henchmen riding east. Haines and his two aides came slowly up the steep path from the barn. A moment later, Lary heard the exhaust of their car as they drove off. The house grew still.

The telephone's sharp clangor startled Day. He wheeled. "What the hell?" he snapped.

Northup grunted. "Forgot to tell you. One of those handymen that came with Haines told me they noticed on their way out here where the wire was down, so they stopped and patched it up. Said it'd been cut, all right. The break was at a place where a pole was down, so the wire was easy for a man to reach. Looks like he played in luck, right from the start."

"Luck, hell!" Day said. "He knew the ground!" Northup lifted the receiver from its hook. "Hello! . . . Oh, hello, Starr. Yeah, this is Northup. What's up now?" There was a pause. Lary could hear the muffled buzzing of Starr's voice across the wire.

"*Shot!?*" Northup's startled word was like an oath. Day stiffened, suddenly alert and tense.

"All right. I'll come right out."

Northup's hand moved very slowly as he lifted the receiver to its hook again. He turned. His face was almost comic in its blank bewilderment.

"What's wrong?"

Northup ran his tongue across dry lips. "Tom McElvey's hurt," he said slowly. "Starr says he accidentally shot himself—last night sometime."

15

NORTHUP set his kit case down on the floor beside Tom McElvey's bed and stood erect again, his hands on his hips, to glower at the patient. McElvey blinked and grinned a little sheepishly. He was a wizened, thin-faced little man, typically Scotch. His shrewd gaze traveled from Northup's face to Day's and back again. The doctor made a gesture of apology.

"Oh, Tom, this is—er—But you know Gary Elliott, of course. Gary, Tom McElvey . . . Now, what's all this I hear about you gettin' shot? Fine goin's on! A man of your age, too! Next thing you'll be tellin' me you didn't know it was loaded!"

McElvey chuckled. "I knew she was loaded all right, Doc. But I didn't think she'd turn on me! My own gun, too, that I've petted and kept greasit all these years! It's scandalous! Turned right around, she did, and bit the hand that's fed her!"

"I heard it was your leg she bit!" Northup

said dryly. He sat down on the bed. "Well, how'd it happen, Tom? The truth, now, mind! Remember an honest confession is good for the soul!"

"The truth is it? And did ye think I'd be tellin' ye a loi? 'Twas this way, Doc. I was settin' up the night with a sick horse—"

Northup's laughter broke explosively. McElvey stared at him. "Sorry, Tom. It's the old, old alibi, then? Only, instead of sittin' up with a sick friend, you were sittin' up with a sick horse."

McElvey frowned, "As I was sayin', I was settin' up with a sick horse. It's that black stud, Doc. I'd hate to lose that horse. Wish ye'd take a look at him, 'fore ye go. Be good practice for ye, too."

McElvey blinked. The score was even now, he felt.

"I told the wife before she left what I was fixin' t' do, so when she got back from town and dinna find me in the hoose it dinna worrit her . . . Weel, come dark, I took me lantern and went to the barn. But just as I'm startin' oot, thinks I, 'Now, this'd be a proper time t' file the trigger-notch on that old gun.' So I straps the old girl on me hip and oot I go, pickin' up the proper tools on the way. And I gets me a box t' set on, and hangs me lantern all nice and cozy, and I starts t' work. I been aimin' t' do this little job for quite a spell. The old gun's seen plenty o' sarvice, but she's lately got t' be a wee mite stiff t' pull. So I takes her apart and starts t' filin' away. It's a real touchy job, ye ken, and I'm for takin' me time. I take her apart and I pull her together again maybe half a dozen times afore I get her just t' me likin'. But finally she's as smooth as silk."

McElvey sighed and shook his head. "Weel, I loaded her up agin and just aboot that time the black was needin' a dose o' medicine, so I lays the old girl on the box I been settin' on and I goes t' work on the black. Only thing I can think of, I must've left her cockit. Car'less o' me, sure; but that must've been the way of it . . . Weel, the black ain't likin' his medicine and, what with me tryin' to force it down him, the box gets upset and—ker-blam!—I'm shot! It scares me so I go right over backwards and crack me head agin a corner of the stall. When I come to agin, it's three o'clock in the mornin'! . . . Well o' course, Mither and the lassie've come home long ago. Mither says she seen a light in the barn and thought I was there all right and she was tired and so she went right t' bed. But, as I was sayin', I come to and feels meself over some and I'm shot right through the thick o' me leg. I manage t' get up somehoo and hobble to the hoose. Got as far as the porch and I was tuckered oot. I sets down right there t' get me wind and right there I falls asleep! Starr found me lyin' there, still sleepin' like a babe, when she come down this mornin'."

Northup nodded and reached out to pull the covers down. "I'll take a look—"

But McElvey clutched the quilt up to his chin. "Awk, mon, take keer! . . . Starr, git ye gone! . . . Losh, Doc, ye fair frightened me!" McElvey's embarrassment lent richness to his burring brogue. "I may be an old mon, Doc, but I got me shame! And I'm mither-nakkid underneath this quilt! I told the wife it wasna safe, an' all. But she refused t' soil me clean ondershirt. She argied, d'ye see, that I'd bleed right through it to the sheet anyway, and there's no need t' be soilin' the both o' them!"

So Starr withdrew and Lary gave his sympathy to the old man and followed her. They walked outside and stood in silence for a time, gazing down the Valley's length toward The Notch. Dry heat poured from a blazing sun and rose again in wavering lines that lent a weird illusion of life and movement to the distant peaks. No breeze stirred anywhere and the white dust hung above the Coronado road, suspended there like a gauzy curtain since Northup's car had lifted it. Day's eyes felt hot. And yet the Valley's green vitality was soothing by comparison.

"If it would only rain." Starr's voice was lustreless, lacking emphasis. She hardly knew that she had spoken. The prayer for rain was an incessant undertone, these days, to all the commonplace affairs of life.

Day nodded but he did not speak. There was a feeling of restraint between them now that he could not define. He wondered if the girl, too, sensed the possibilities in Tom McElvey's accident. But it was an accident, he thought. It must have been.

"I didn't try, last night, to tell you how much I sympathize with you . . . about your friend. He must have loved you very much, Gary, to give his life for you so gallantly."

"'Greater love—'" The obvious quotation died unfinished on Day's lip. He could not talk about Greer yet; not in a sentimental vain, at least. The thing was still too near. He waited till the tension in his throat relaxed.

"I fired Red Vale this mornin'," he said slowly. "Vale and all the rest of them. I'll have to hire a whole new crew."

Starr must have understood his reticence for she accepted the change of subject instantly. "I'm glad of that," she said. "I never liked those men; I don't know why. . . . What caused it, so suddenly?"

He told her a flat, uncolored narrative. But he did not repeat Vale's half-spoken reference to names. "I was on edge," he said. "I lost my head. But I'm not regrettin' it. The man put me in mind of a surly dog."

"He's dangerous," Starr said. "You've made a dangerous enemy . . . Be careful, won't you, Gary? Don't ride alone. And—don't go armed. I know you hope to find the—murderer, but—Red Vale is a gunman. One of the few still left. And your wearing arms would simply give him an excuse to kill you."

She saw his withdrawal, the sharper, harder angle of his jaw. The change was barely perceptible, perhaps, but it was there. It was in his voice as well. "I'm not a tenderfoot," he said.

"I've fired a gun a time or two myself . . . But I'll keep off the ridges when I can."

Wisely, Starr let it go at that. She had lived much with men; knew something of their stubborn, rigid codes. This man would not seek trouble with Red Vale, she knew; but neither would he swerve an inch from his determined course on Vale's account. That knowledge frightened her and made her proud.

She said, "I phoned the MacGregor boys this morning. Told them to drive my cattle home. And that reminds me. Whoever's in charge of them for you will want authority to give them up."

He nodded. "I'll phone Brett Randall now."

She caught his arm. "Don't tell him that you've sold the stock back to me, Gary. Just tell him that you're putting the cattle on the Valley range to keep them fat."

Her urgent tone brought an inquiring glance from him and Starr's eyes fell. But she looked up at him again. "Please, Gary. I—I have a reason, really. Do as I say?"

"Why, sure."

But the dry humor of the thing appealed to him. That Starr's quick solicitude over the so-far intangible threat of Red Vale's enmity should be followed now by a request that would hold over him the sharper sword, unquestionably real, that had snuffed out Greer's life last night—that incongruity struck him as humorous. For just so long as Brett Randall stood in ignorance of the final consummation of Day's purchase of The Notch, so long would Day's life stand a barrier against Brett Randall's greed. Once Randall knew that the deal was complete, that threat would be removed. For there was no slightest doubt in Lary's mind but that last night's attack had grown out of his talk with Randall and his fighting man. Even while the echoes of those first two shots still rang, Day's mind had pictured Marsden as the man behind the gun. It was so logical as to be almost inevitable. Even the proof that Marsden could not have fired those shots left Day's major premise still unchanged. He had erred, perhaps, in visualizing Marsden as the tool; but he was certain that Brett Randall was the mind behind whatever tool was used. And Randall would try again.

But that, he knew, was a conclusion that had not occurred to Starr. He walked back into the house and called Randall. The MacGregors had been there, Randall said, and were waiting for confirmation of their right to move the stock. Randall had tried to get in touch with Day at the Broken Bar but had failed. Yes, he would allow the removal of the cattle although he would strongly advise against the move. The market—

Day hung up. Northup came out of Tom McElvey's room as he finished and walked with Lary to the porch. He nodded reassuringly at Starr. "Old Tom'll be all right," he said. "Keep him in bed, that's all. Rest is what he needs. He's lost considerable blood, but there's no serious damage done . . . Come along, young man. I haven't been away from my practice as long as this before in years. It's a little humiliatin', really, that there hasn't been a general alarm and a widespread search for me! Seems as if maybe my patients can get along without me, after all. I better get back before *they* discover that! . . . bye, Starr. Tell Mother Mac she can put a nightshirt on him now. The hole's plugged up."

But he was not so jovial once he and Day were alone in the car. He shot a covert, sidelong glance at Lary as they rolled through the gate.

"Sort of a coincidence, eh, Starr's callin' me

right after you warned me to look out for a mysterious gunshot wound?"

Day shrugged but did not speak. His silence displeased Northup vaguely. "What'd you think of Tom's story, anyway? You satisfied with it?"

"Why not?"

"Don't be so damn dense! Here's a shootin' scrape with one of the shooters gettin' away supposedly wounded. That same night, a careful man like Tom McElvey gets shot in the leg, by accident. McElvey is an old-time guntoter; used to guns since he was knee-high to a calf. Damn funny, him layin' a loaded gun down cocked, if you ask me!"

"I didn't ask you," Day said. "Suspicious cuss, ain't you? Not that I didn't think of those same things, myself.... It might've happened, though, just like he said it did. No doubt it did happen that way. A man can be careful all his life and then do a downright careless thing that trips him up. Like me, this mornin'. I've been weighin' my words and thinkin' before I took a step for weeks. Then I fork a buckin' horse and plumb forget that I ain't at a rodeo! ... Anyway, why would Tom McElvey shoot at me?"

"There's an answer to that, too; or might

be," Northup said. "We know that the McElvey family didn't exactly approve of Starr's visitin' you last night. Witness Mother Mac's attitude. And Mother Mac was real upset when Starr didn't get back to town just when she thought she ought to, too. Seems almost like the old lady might've *expected* trouble . . . Suppose Mother Mac ain't the only one that was chaperonin' Starr last night. You were sittin' on the porch, you said. Nice evenin', too. Pretty sunset . . . Son, did you make any pass at Starr last night that Tom McElvey might've sort of —misconstrued?"

"I certainly did not!" Day said indignantly. But then he flushed. "Well, not before the shootin', anyway. I—Say! What is this, anyway? The third degree?"

Northup chuckled. "Not *before* the shootin', eh? But afterward . . . H'mm . . . Well, what happened *after* the shootin' couldn't very well be the reason *for* the shootin', could it now? So maybe Tom was tellin' us the truth, at that."

"Some people do," Day said sarcastically. "It's a quaint, old-fashioned custom, sure, but some folks seem to cling to it."

Northup frowned at him. "What the devil are you talkin' about, anyway?"

"Truth-tellin'."

"Oh, that . . . Why, yes. And then, again, some people don't."

The subject dried up automatically and Northup drove in silence after that until they passed The Notch. His voice was casual when he spoke at last. "So you're in love with her."

Day shot an angry glance at him, then faced the front, his face expressionless. "Suppose I am?"

"Hell, I'm not blamin' you! I've loved Starr Landerson myself, ever since I spanked the first breath into her. Lord how she bawled! . . . What do you aim to do about it, son?"

"What *can* I do?"

But Northup could not answer that. No more could Day. What with Greer's death and all this morning's happenings, his mind had been too full till now to grasp the situation that confronted him. He faced it squarely now and it disheartened him. Belle Turner, Gary Elliott, Brett Randall, Vale—the whole thing was a hopeless jumble. Its complications were too numerous. It had been no simple game when he came into it, this masquerade, and its complexities had multiplied. Now, Pop Greer's death had stripped the glamour off of it; had left it bleak and ugly, meaningless.

"But I'll go through with it," Day thought. "I promised Pop."

He was reminded then of Greer's last words. "Star cattle in the hills." He voiced that thought to Northup. "Of course, Pop might've seen a bunch of strays. But that wasn't the idea I got from what he said."

The doctor frowned. "It don't sound like strays to me, either," he said. "In the first place, Tom McElvey is a damned good cattleman. And, in the second place, he's Scotch! Any Starr-branded strays that got away from him would be few and far between. Starr's lost a lot of stuff of late to rustlers. But why would they be holdin' them?"

Day shrugged. "That's somethin' else to be found out, I reckon. I got a hunch—somethin' I heard about a creek dryin' up unexpectedly. I've got some chores to do first; roundin' up the Broken Bar stuff and shovin' 'em onto the Valley range, for one thing. But after that I aim to take a jaunt up through the hills."

Northup nodded. "When you do that," he said, "you watch your step. One way and another, you've made yourself a lot of enemies. Remember that."

Northup would have driven on to the Broken Bar but Lary called a halt in town. "I've got to make arrangements for Pop's funeral," he said. "And, anyway, I might as well buy me a car. I can't depend on a busy man like you to taxi me around."

The car he bought was no such gorgeous chariot as the yellow roadster he had wrecked, but it was staunch and serviceable. He bought it second hand and paid for it out of the billfold he had found in Elliott's clothes. But he did not pay for Pop's funeral. He would pay for that later, out of money that was his own.

The afternoon was well advanced when he drove out of town. He had met the MacGregor boys—three brothers; lean, dour, blue-eyed men—and watched them start the cattle back toward The Notch. And he had hired four men to take the place of those he had dismissed, selecting them with careful reference to the three MacGregors' sparsely worded and unwillingly obtained advice. Angus MacGregor, eldest of the brothers, had protested hurriedly when Lary would have hired more men.

"Four's plenty, mon!" he said. "Ye'll not be

needin' a topheavy crew, ye ken; not with the stuff all bunched around The Notch already. Ye ain't the cows ye once had, either, I'm remindin' ye."

The glance accompanying the last remark had held reproof and Lary smiled, recalling it. Evidently Gary Elliott's record as a cattleman was not an enviable one; at least, not in the judgment of the three MacGregor boys.

A freight train lumbered out of town ahead of Day and he slowed down to let its racket pass. But the road ran parallel to the tracks for three miles or so and he overtook the train as it slowed almost to a halt and crept at a snail's pace across a tall trestle spanning one of Sweetwater's tributaries. Repairs were in progress on the bridge and Lary remembered vaguely having seen a crew of men at work when he passed by with Northup earlier in the day.

The railroad angled to the south beyond the bridge, beginning its long circuit to swing past the foot of the Antelopes. Just short of the point where the dirt road branched steeply back toward the Broken Bar, a furrowed scar along the shoulder of the road caught Lary's eye and he halted there and climbed out of the car. Tracks slanted off the pavement into a jungle of tall weeds; but the tread patterns of those tracks had been most carefully wiped out. The tracks came up onto the road again beyond the thicket, but there, too, the treads were smeared and meaningless; not erased by hand as the others had been, but made by skidding, spinning wheels as if a car had lurched along the slope in headlong haste. Day remembered the crescendo roar of a motor at open throttle and the clash of gears as someone drove a car away just after Pop Greer's death. He frowned and shrugged. The ground was trampled here and many boot tracks stood out clearly in the torn-up soil, but Lary paid no heed to them. The man who drove the car had been a careful man and he had left no sign. But there had been others here since then; men who were not careful. These tracks were left, Day knew, by Haines and his deputies.

"If there ever was anything to find," he thought, "it's not here now."

16

THEY buried Pop Greer the following day in the little cemetery overlooking Sweetwater Creek where village lawns gave way to open range, to rolling prairies carpeted with sweet brown grass and tufted here and there with sage and cactus clumps. It was a simple ceremony and Lary chose a morning hour for it in order to avoid the curious. But Starr was there, and Mrs. McElvey, and Northup and the three MacGregor boys. Day felt their sympathy and was grateful for it. But as he left that open grave he felt, as he had never felt so utterly before, alone and bitterly bereft.

Northup rode back to town with him and he must have sensed Day's loneliness for he insisted that Lary stop and share a drink with him. In the privacy of the big, clean room behind the office in the doctor's house, Day found an outlet for his grief in words. He took the glass that Northup offered him, and, as they drank, he talked. Not as he had talked to Blaine that day—it seemed a long, long time ago—when they had halted at Apache Tanks, for he had talked to Blaine about himself. It was Greer he talked of now, painting in terse, disconnected strokes a portrait of a kindly man against the clear, strong canvas of the west. He used few adjectives, for this was not a eulogy; but out of homely incident the pattern grew until the listener felt an intimate, sure knowledge of the man Pop Greer had been.

And Northup gained as well, a clearer knowledge of the speaker himself. For, all unwittingly, Day's own portrait showed clearly in the scenes he drew; and Northup listened while a warm contentment grew in him; for Day's words justified the doctor's own instinctive estimate.

"So you see, Pop wasn't just a friend to me. He was a father, and a teacher, and a playmate, and—a guide."

Northup nodded thoughtfully. "And there's his epitaph," he said.

He stood up suddenly and laid his hand on Lary's arm. "I know," he said. "You feel—alone. But son, you're not. You've got a life before you here; friends, future, happiness." Day shook his head. "Friends, yes. There's you, and Starr. As for the rest of it . . ." he shrugged. "My future isn't here. Nor is my happiness. I'm an imposter here; a fraud."

Northup's big voice had a solemn timbre when he spoke again. "I'm not a judge of right or wrong," he said. "But I've thought considerable about your situation here. Last night I laid awake . . ." He shrugged. "Starr's dear to me. Knowin' how you feel toward her—I added that in, too. And I got an answer. I don't say it's the right answer, you understand. But it seems right to me. It goes like this."

He glanced at Day and looked away. "The first thing is, you didn't kill that Turner girl. Partly, I'm taking your word for that. Partly, too, I'm taking what I know of Gary Elliott. Because, if you didn't kill her, Gary must've been the guilty one. And—it's the sort of thing he might've done. A sneakin', cornered-rat sort of thing. They talk a lot these days about heredity. And about environment. But Gary had good parentage and a good home, yet he was bad. . . . All right. You say you're an imposter here. Suppose you are. A good man in a bad man's shoes! He's dead, and rightly so. And you're alive, and innocent."

Day stiffened as the doctor's meaning became clear to him. "But, Doc—!"

"Wait, son. Let me get through with this. In two weeks here you've done more good than Gary Elliott has ever done—would ever do. You're takin' Gary's place ain't hurtin' *him*. It ain't hurtin' anyone. Why not go through with it?"

Day gasped. "But Starr—and Elliott's property! You're jokin', Doc; the thing's impossible!"

"It's worked all right, so far. Why wouldn't it go right on workin'? Why not marry Starr, if she'll have you? You ain't good enough for her, I'll admit; but if you can make her love you, she'll never think of that! No woman ever does. . . . As to Elliott's property, you take that, too! It ain't so much, from what I hear. Gary frittered his inheritance away, or most of it. He did his best to ruin what was left of it, too; the Broken Bar. It would have been ruined eventually. Grab onto it! Rebuild the Broken Bar. Help Starr create a paradise up there above The Notch. And build that dam! If you do that, or one damn tenth of it, you'll justify whatever wrong you may have done! You've got a chance to do a miracle! With water, which that dam would provide, this whole, bleak, thirsty range would blossom like a rose. . . . Why, hell! The crime would be in turnin' down your opportunity, not in acceptin' it!"

Northup paused, a little breathless from the fervor of his argument. Day said, "You make it sound all right, at that!"

"That's what I'm drivin' at. It's—right! Or, anyway, it sure seems right to me."

But Lary shook his head. "You're forgettin' that I'm a fugitive," he said. "I'm innocent. But, innocent or guilty, I'm wanted by the law. One slip and I'd be—gallows meat. And even if that wasn't true, even if I could prove my innocence, I couldn't live a lie—with Starr. . . . And, if I had to live *without* her, I'd want to get away from *here*. . . . So, either way, that licks your argument."

"Tell her, then! Tell Starr the truth, if you must! I'll bet on her to see it like I do!"

But Lary shook his head again. He stood up wearily and turned toward the door. "I'm grateful, Doc, for all you've done for me. Talkin' to you has made it easier. I've still got things to do here, and—I want to do 'em. Find

Pop's murderer, for one. But after that . . . oh, Mexico, perhaps; some place like that."

"You think it over, anyway," Northup insisted stubbornly.

And, despite his own conviction in the case, the doctor's argument took a tenacious grip on Lary's mind. He thrust it aside, only to find it returning again and again to plague him. The reasoning seemed sound, yet something deep inside of him insisted that the thing was wrong. He even tried to sneer and shrug his scruples off, for the plan combined two lures for him: Starr Landerson, and with her, a rich, full life of real accomplishment. The possibilities for development latent in Star Valley range alone held forth the prospect of a lifetime of enthralling and productive work; work for which Day longed with a fierce lust. The love of land was strong in him and here was land on which a man could build an earthy paradise. But the scruples clung persistently and would not be cast aside.

Following his talk with Northup, Lary flung himself into his work with a grim fervor that was designed to fill his mind too full for either grief or thought. Riding as foreman with the men he had hired to replace Vale and Vale's three satellites, he spent four strenuous days in rounding up the gaunt, depleted Elliott herds. Bit by bit he poured the gatherings through The Notch into Star Valley and, on that sweet range, the hungry cattle thrived and flourished and increased in weight with a rapidity that was almost visible.

But work failed utterly to still the siren song that filled his mind. The parched, bleak land itself was a constant reminder. Its barrenness cried out to him. He held the key that could unlock the vast fertility that lay beneath that blackened mask. Water! A dam to store up an unfailing reservoir behind The Notch; ditches, veining all this lower range with their life-giving streams. The thought obsessed him; haunted him with a peculiar sense of guilt.

He did his work, however, with a dispatch and skill that pleased and puzzled the MacGregor boys as well as his own crew. As the Broken Bar stock came through The Notch, the MacGregors scattered them so that there might be no concentration that would overburden any section of the Valley range. And, when the task was done, Day, working with the MacGregors under Tom McElvey's jealous eye, estimated that the range would still be lightly stocked and that not even a continuation of the drought for six months more would seriously damage it.

"And after that," McElvey pointed out with pride, "we'll have the hay. Enough of it for six months more."

"But it'll rain," Day said. "Good God! It's got to rain sometime! It always does!"

Angus MacGregor smiled cannily. "It's an ill wind, though, that blows nobody good. If we dinna get the rain we're fair sure t' get a nice beef market. There's bound t' be a scarcity, and the best time t' have an oversupply o' anything, ye ken, is when it's scarce!"

Day shrugged. "We won't have such an oversupply though, unless the boom comes soon. Starr will have to sell her stuff inside of ninety days to enable her to meet that mortgage. Even that soon, though, I figure she'll get a profit. The Broken Bar stuff can wait. Sooner or later prices are bound to rise. Starr's to get a percentage on the increase, whether in weight, value or calf-crop, on the Broken Bar stock as payment for grazing privileges, so she'll share in any such variation in the market. I'm leavin' my crew with you, MacGregor, to help handle the stuff. They'll take their orders from you, or from McElvey; either one.

McElvey glanced at Day suspiciously. "You ain't leavin' us?" he said.

"Long enough to do some chores, that's all," Day said.

He left the conference with a sense of freedom from the duties that had held him in unwilling check these past four days. Freedom to carry out the plans Greer's death had automatically mapped out for him. Primarily, he meant to find Greer's murderer. Just how that might be done, he did not know; but there were certain questions in his mind, the answers to which might lead him to the man he sought. Who, other than Marsden and Brett Randall, was interested in his purchase of The Notch? Why were Marsden and Randall interested? And where had Marsden gone the night when Greer was killed.

Marsden's continued absence, too, fired Day's curiosity. Five men—Marsden, Vale, Joe Travis, Tommy Ladd and Buck Dupree—had disappeared out of the ken of the Coronado folk since Pop Greer's death and Lary wondered why. Their going was too apt, he thought, for mere coincidence.

Then, too, there was the matter of the cattle Greer had seen back in the hills. That mystery took second place in Lary's mind and he saw little importance in it other than a possible minor increase in the tally of Starr's herd. But it kept recurring in his consciousness with tantalizing frequency.

The conference in McElvey's room had begun just after the completion of the mid-day meal and Lary stepped out now into bright heat that struck him like a blow. His car stood in the blue shadow of trees below the house and, as he came down from the porch, he saw that it was occupied. Starr's shining head lay motionless against the cushioned seat-back and thin, spinning rings of smoke rose lazily to form a halo near it. Day's footsteps lagged a little as he neared the car. He had seen Starr frequently in the course of his work these past four days, but there had been no return to the calm, easy friendliness that he had felt in her the night of Pop Greer's death. Lary felt that Starr had been avoiding him; had found, without the slightest doubt, a reason to support that fact. It seemed to him that she must be taking this as the easiest means of preventing a recurrence of his slip that night.

"She needn't worry," he thought resentfully. "I told her the truth, but I'm not fool enough to make the same mistake again."

She turned her head to smile at him. "I'm learning to blow smoke rings, Gary . . . Why so glum?"

He did not speak. She sat up suddenly and stared at him. "What's wrong?"

"Nothing wrong. Surprised, is all, to find you here. You've been avoiding me."

He had not meant to say that. Saying it made him angry at himself. He had meant to force himself to anger her.

"I've kept out of the way," Starr said quietly. "I've let you do your work. And—yes, I have avoided you. I wanted time to . . . think."

Her obvious meaning startled him. Anger drained out of him, leaving a sort of panic in its place. To love and lose was bad enough. He dared not face the possibility of knowing that he might have won.

He said, "I've got to go."

She nodded. "I'm going with you. That's why I'm waiting here. The surveyors finished their job last night and I'm going in to get their report and pay them off. We'll just conclude our little deal at the same time, if you like."

She moved aside as he got in, making room for him. "I was going in with Mother Mac, but I sent her on alone. Poor dear! She hates to drive a car. But I wanted to talk to you. . . . You might show a bit of enthusiasm, Gary!"

The motor roared and gears clashed angrily from Day's rough handling. "I'm glad to have you, of course." His tone was roughly casual but the car lurched drunkenly as he changed gears and charged the gate. He did not look at her. "What do you want to talk about?"

She waited until the car stopped skidding after its tight turn into the dusty road. "Do you always drive like this?" she asked. "Or is it a special demonstration for my benefit?"

"Sorry. I was thinkin' of something else."

"Oh. . . . Gary, I want you to record the deed to the land as soon as we've signed it. Will you? Today, I mean."

He glanced at her, relieved by the turn their talk was taking. He had expected her to speak of his "I love you, Starr," that night of Pop Greer's death. This was in the nature of a reprieve. His voice was not so curt this time. "Why all the rush?"

"I was a fool to want you to keep our deal a secret, Gary. I see that now. Whoever shot at you that night did it with the idea that, by killing you, he could prevent your buying this land and thereby prevent me from meeting my mortgage. Keeping it a secret simply prolongs the danger for you. So long as someone thinks the deal isn't complete, he's got the incentive to try again. I knew that all along, of course; but I simply didn't think it through. I thought —Well, I really thought I was doing you a favor, Gary. I know better now. You'll do it, won't you? Record the deed, so anyone who's interested will know that it's all settled?"

She did not mention his check. She still held that, and would not cash it yet. In that respect, at least, she was certain still that she had done the proper thing.

"Of course," he said. "I was goin' on out home, but I can spare the time, I reckon, to record a deed. That won't take long." He shrugged. "You needn't have worried, though. Whoever took that shot at me seems to have dropped the idea. I've passed a lot of likely spots for murder since, but here I am. Seems like he was right easily discouraged, that hombre."

"It's only been four days," Starr said. "Don't get careless, Gary, yet, I—" Her voice broke a little. She let the sentence go unfinished and turned her face from him.

The pause was eloquent. It was Day's cue to say, "Would you care much, Starr?" And he knew in his heart how she would answer him. But he did not speak. Blood pounded in his temples with an aching beat. He dared not look at her. He told himself, "*It's all a lie; a fraud. I've used another man's name and another man's money to make a grandstand play that's sort of dazzled her. That's all it is.*"

The moment passed. They ran suddenly between the high walls of The Notch, through deep shadow over which the sun's rays sloped like a golden canopy. After that respite, the plunge into the glaring heat that lay upon the Coronado range was a breathtaking shock. It seemed a drier heat, somehow, than that above The Notch. There was an odor here, faint but tangible, like that which clings to old ashes. Grass, cropped to its very roots by hungry stock, had left the land naked so that searching winds had blown the soil clear of the roots and now the roots themselves lay black and burned upon the hardened crust. The sight was sickening. Day pushed the car to better speed, welcoming the motor's noise that masked but did not break a silence that had stretched his nerves almost to the breaking point. He was glad when they reached the town at last and halted in front of the building housing the county offices. Those last few miles had seemed interminable.

In the surveyor's office, Starr paid her fee for services. The man in charge was almost fawningly polite. "We left a map, together with a description of the property, with Dr. Northup, as you instructed us. However, I have a copy here if you would care to see it."

"Just the description, now," Starr said. "I'm drawing up a deed."

The task took longer, however, than Day had anticipated. At Starr's suggestion, they crossed the street to Northup's office to wait there while the deed was written up. There, again, Day felt the silence grow unbearable. He scanned the papers in the doctor's waiting room; found them yellowing with age. He paced the floor. Starr read a woman's magazine. Her placidness built up a towering rage in Day. An hour passed.

Northup joined them finally, and soon after that, Starr's lawyer brought the filled-in deeds. The surveyor spread his maps on Northup's desk, but Lary hardly glanced at them. There was a little flurry while signatures were affixed and copies of the deed exchanged.

Starr said, "I want this deed recorded immediately."

The lawyer bowed. "I will attend to that," he said. "At once!"

It was over finally. Northup, the lawyer, the surveyor, gone. Day stood up thankfully and snatched his hat. Starr stood over Northup's desk, bent forward slightly as she scanned the maps.

Day said, "Well, I'll be goin' now. So long. . . ."

But Starr seemed not to hear. She said, "Why, here's a funny thing, Gary. According to this map, I own—or used to own—that ridge on either side of The Notch. I didn't know that. Dad must have bought it to protect the site of his beloved dam."

She turned to him. "You've bought more land than you thought, Gary. All the land south of a given line—that's the way the agreement read and that's the instructions I gave for the drawing of the deed. You remember that day when I took you up there? You asked me then who owned that ridge. I didn't know."

Day said, "Good God!"

She stared at him. But Lary had forgotten her. One simple fact—the ownership of that bleak ridge—jerked other facts into an interlocking pattern in his mind. The prospect shaft he had seen on the ridge that day; Greer's mention of a rumor that someone had struck pay-dirt near here; the presence of a mining man—"name of Calahan," Pop Greer had said —in Coronado; Brett Randall's frantic effort to obtain The Star; all these were one! Day wheeled toward the door.

Starr caught his arm. "What is it, Gary? Tell me!"

He said, "There's a gold mine on that ridge, that's all! That's why Brett Randall wanted it. I'll stop that man before he gets that deed recorded. Our deal is off!"

He would have gone but she held on to him. "No, Gary! The deal's complete! You can't back out—"

"But, don't you see? A *mine*—it may be worth millions! It may not be worth a dime, too; but we'll make sure. This way, I might be robbin' you."

She shook her head. "We made the deal in ignorance of the mine, if there *is* a mine. It was a deal that saved my life, financially. If you make millions out of it, that's your good luck. I'll be *glad*, Gary. Because then you'll build your dam."

He shook his head, half frantic with the need for haste. "But damn it, Starr, I won't be buildin' any dam! I can't! Because I'm not— my name ain't Gary Elliott—"

She laid her hands across his lips and smiled. "I know," she said. "I've known for quite a while. You're Lary Day."

17

DAY stared at her. "You knew?" he said. His mind felt numb. The little world he had built up so carefully had crashed. He said, slowly, "Northup told you!"

"Yes. But I knew, already; almost from the start. Even when you were sick I sensed—something. It puzzled me. I kept adding up things I saw in you that weren't like—him. You love the land and Gary hated it. Your helping me—he never would've done a thing like that. So, finally, I was sure that you *weren't* him. It was on the way to Broken Bar, that night I dined with you, that I made up my mind definitely. Then—I passed Pop Greer. I almost recognized him; not quite, because he'd shaved his mustache off. But, when you came down to greet me, before I got out of my car, it all came clear to me. I remembered how you walked toward me like that after you rode that horse at the Sedalia rodeo. And then I knew who Pop Greer was, too."

Day nodded. "I should've known I couldn't get away with it."

But Starr went on. "It was after that—two days ago—that Northup talked to me. You mustn't blame him, Lary. I made him, really. He knew I knew before he talked. He wants you to—go on with it, you see? He thought you would if I—That is—Why don't you, Lary? It's so—*right!*"

He said, "You want me to do *that?*"

She nodded and her eyes were bright with sudden tears.

He jerked away. "Don't tempt me, Starr!" Swift anger flared in him and he turned, facing her, his body taut. "Good God! You ask me to stay here—me! A fugitive! Sentenced to be hung! Stay here, where I'd be close to you—lovin' you—! Don't be a fool!"

Starr faced him steadily. "You're not a murderer, Lary. I never needed proof of that. But if I had, your coming here was proof enough. No guilty man would ever take a risk like that."

He flung away from her, striding back to stand before a window looking out into an empty yard. She followed him.

"You might be fair, Lary," she said softly.

"You said you—loved me, you know. You meant that, didn't you? And doesn't that give me some—rights?" She saw him stiffen; saw the muscles on his jaw stand out until the skin went white. She said, "I love you, too, you see. If you take Gary's place or not—that doesn't matter. The other thing—your being a fugitive —we'd face that together. Don't you see?"

The fight went out of him, deflating him. His shoulders sagged. He turned and groped for her. She gave a small glad cry and came into his arms. He held her hungrily and pressed his face into her hair.

"I can't fight *you*," he murmured brokenly. "I love you so!"

So, moments later, Northup found them, locked in each other's arms, and his deep chuckle startled them apart. He said, "Well, now you two are showin' sense! Congratulations, both o' you! I knew she'd bring you to it, son. Old Dan Cupid himself; that's me!"

He beamed expansively and flung an arm around each one of them. "Makes me feel young again, this does! Now, maybe, I can get some sleep! I been layin' awake nights long enough, worryin' about you young fools!

What's it goin' to be, Starr? Mrs. Gary Elliott, or Mrs. Lary Day?"

"I wouldn't know," Starr said. "Or care! It's up to him."

"It'll be Mrs. Lary Day, if anything," Day said. "I'll never marry her while that murder is hangin' over me, and in order to clear myself I'll have to step out of Elliott's shoes. But—that's all right." He glanced at Starr and smiled. "I'll clear myself, all right. I couldn't fail; not now."

"Of course you will!" Northup's big voice boomed resoundingly. "Only I wouldn't rush things too much, Lary."

He paused and grinned at Starr. "Gary—Lary. Nice, their bein' similar, eh, Starr? Make it easy to remember, sort of."

He turned to Day again. "What I'm gettin' at is this. If you step out of character now, Randall's goin' to fight your deal with Starr. But, if you wait until Starr's paid Randall off —got him out of the picture, so to speak—I figure the deal'll stand unless somebody makes a kick, anyway; and the only ones apt to make such a kick are the principals involved. Said principals bein' Starr, here, and Gary's heirs.

Starr ain't goin' to make a kick, that's a cinch. And Gary's heirs, whoever they are—"

"Won't either!" Lary said. "Good Lord! That deed!" He glanced shamefacedly at Starr.

"It's too late now," she said. "And, anyway, who cares? It was—worth a gold mine or two, wasn't it?"

Day's answer left her radiant; but it embarrassed Northup and he turned, grumbling, and would have left. Starr called him back. "You'll have to bear with us," she said. "It's your own fault! . . . About the deed. You tell him, Lary."

Day talked briefly and Northup listened, nodding now and then as he found answers to the questions that had troubled all of them. Day finished and the doctor frowned.

"So that's the reason Randall was so set on ownin' the Star! And you've done Elliott's heirs an even bigger favor than you intended doin' 'em, eh, Lary?" He shrugged. "Well, you can't make omelets without breakin' eggs, they say. You'll have The Star all free and clear, anyway. And that's somethin'! Judgin' by Lary's remarks on that subject, I ain't so sure he ain't marryin' you to get The Star, anyway, young lady!"

Starr made a face at him. "He is! And whether you spell it with one R or two, the results are the same!"

An hour passed unnoticed as they talked and it was only the arrival of Mrs. McElvey to take Starr home that ended it. Day's good-bye kiss to Starr left Mother Mac aghast and Lary beat a hasty retreat before her wrath found words. He heard Northup's deep, uproarious laughter following him, and grinned. It was the gayest hour he had known in weeks. And certainly the happiest.

He walked directly to the Coronado House. Starr's nonchalant acceptance of the loss of a gold mine—if there *was* a gold mine—was admirable, perhaps, but certainly impractical; and Day believed that it could be saved for her.

"Buyin' an irrigation project was one thing," he told himself. "Buyin' it saved Starr, and ownin' it did her little good. She lacked the capital to develop it. But a gold mine—that's somethin' else again! If it's any good at all, she could sell it, or sell an interest in it, for enough to pay Randall and have somethin' left. And the transfer of title to the land ain't legal, because I had no right to sell the cattle used to pay for it. Admittin' that might put me in a legal jam, but—it's an idea, anyway."

A fat man in a wilted linen suit heaved up from a chair in the lobby in response to Lary's inquiry at the desk for a man named Calahan.

"I'm Calahan," he puffed. "Sit down! God-a'mighty, ain't it hot! Boy, bring two more long tall lemonades.... Lemonades! That's what prohibition's done for this damn country! Forced lemonades down our long-sufferin' throats! ... Elliott, eh? Gary Elliott, ain't it? Own the Broken Bar. I've heard o' you. What can I do for you?"

Day sat down. The lobby was empty but he kept his voice down low. "You ever know a man named Greer? Pop Greer?"

"Hell, yes!" The fat man grinned. "Seen him here just the other day. Wait! He said his name was—Damn! Now I've give the ol' coot away! Hope you're a friend o' his?"

"I am. But Pop Greer's dead." Day cut the fat man's sympathetic gesture short. Calahan had heard that someone had been killed, of course; but he had never connected the fact with Greer. "Pop told me you were here; said you were investigating a rumored strike near here. You bought a mine from Pop, didn't you?"

"I did! A good one, too, even if he did jack the price up on me! Shrewd old codger, Greer! Had a heart as big as a barrel, though. You know anything about his rumored mine?"

"I own it."

"The hell you do!" The fat man chuckled wheezily. "Well, I always said the way t' do business was t' set tight and let business come t' you! I sat tight, and drank lemonade, and—here you are!"

Day grinned. "How much do you know?"

Calahan grunted and made an explosive gesture with his fat, red hands. A boy set two glasses on the window sill beside them and Calahan waited until they were alone again.

"Just this: First, though, let me explain. The market price o' gold has been skyrocketin'. You know that. Producin' gold is our business. Damn profitable business now, too, providin' we can get the stuff. Other companies like us are in the same fix. Bad business, my tellin' you how bad we want somethin' you got, but let that ride. All right. All's fair in love and war, ain't it? Well, this is war! Maybe it ain't good ethics, but it's damn good business t' keep an eye on your competitors. We do! Never mind how we got it, but we got word that one of our competitors was negotiatin' for somethin' here. I beat it out here to do some snoopin'. As a snooper, I'm a big success. Folks always trust a fat man."

The man's speech came in explosive little bursts, like firecrackers on a string.

"But I couldn't learn a thing, at first. Didn't know who to approach. Knew if I made a fuss —let folks know I was biddin'—the price'd climb. So I waited. Always have been good at waitin'. Run into Pop Greer and thought he might help. Now, Pop is dead, you say. . . . That's all there is. It's your turn now. You talk."

Day said, "How much did your competitor intend to pay? Or do you know?"

"Smart boy! I'll tell you, though. A million, cash."

Day caught his breath. The fat man grinned.

"Think I'm a fool, don't you, t'tell you that? I ain't. I know the company that made that offer. If they say a million, they know what they're doin'. It's probably worth more. If it ain't, that's their lookout. I haven't made an offer, have I? Won't either, till I know what I'm doin'."

Day nodded and stood up. "I wasn't mistakin' you for a fool," he said sincerely. "Mr. Calahan, you keep right on sittin' tight. I said I owned that mine. I do, in a way. But never mind that now. You can depend on this: the mine won't change hands without my say-so. And when I'm ready to say so, I'll say it to you."

Calahan nodded. "Fair enough," he said. "I'll string along with you. I like your looks."

"In the meantime," Day said, "you might send for your experts to look things over, so you'll be prepared to make an offer when the time comes. When they get here, I'll show 'em where to look."

"Right. Shoot a wire t' the home office tonight. Glad t've met you, Elliott. Buy bonds with that million, y'hear? If you get it! Gov'ment bonds. Don't say I didn't warn you!"

Day grinned and walked out to his car. It had been a short, terse interview but it had left his head spinning. A million dollars! Money to clear the Star of debt, restock it, irrigate, develop it into a paradise. And he had robbed Starr Landerson of that!

"I'll get it back for her," he thought. "I'll break that deed. What's a little thing like forgery to a man already sentenced to be hung?"

The westbound passenger train overtook him as he drove toward the Broken Bar and he watched it slow almost to a full stop before it crept out gingerly upon the weakened bridge. That was the train Lem Marsden had taken out of Coronado the night of Pop Greer's death and Lary wondered where the man was now and if he would return. The thought of Marsden sobered him.

"I've got things to do," he thought. "A lot of things. And not much time."

Night fell before he reached the point from which his road forked back toward the Broken Bar, and when he reached the ranch the house was dark. He swung in close beside the porch and cut the motor off. The car lights blinked out, leaving utter blackness until his eyes became accustomed to the starlit dark. The place seemed dead, unoccupied. He wondered where Chang might have gone.

The floorboards echoed hollow beneath his tread as he climbed up the steps and crossed the porch. He frowned and struck a match. The silence struck him with a strange uneasiness. The flaring match showed him a lamp upon a table in the center of the vast front room and he crossed toward it, conscious of a prickling dread that made the nerves across his back contract and cringe. "Scared of the dark!" he thought. "Like some small boy!" But it was real.

The lamp-wick caught and burned in a blue, smoky flame. He set the chimney over it. The flame steadied and suffused the room with light. Day shrugged and swung his right hand up towards his hat. "*Odd how an empty house feels spooky in the dark,*" he thought.

And, back of him, close to the door, a floorboard creaked.

"Don't move!"

The curt command cracked out with startling violence. Day waited, motionless. The man behind him chuckled gloatingly.

"Right smart o' me, Elliott? I knowed you'd strike a light; knowed you'd reach up that-a-way t' get your hat. I figgered it all out. I didn't want t' kill you suddenlike. I want t' talk some first."

Day's fingers twitched and tightened on his hat. He knew that voice, yet its identity eluded him. But he could feel the hate, the deadly threat in it. He heard the scrape of footsteps as the man came closer cautiously. He glimpsed the gnarled brown hand that snatched his gun out of its sheath; heard the man behind him sigh with gratified relief.

"Now you can turn around, I reckon. Don't make no sudden movements, though. Sit yonder in that chair."

Day turned. A small, bent figure stood against the wall across the room from him, a leveled gun held rigidly, waist-high. The thing was like a picture taken literally out of the past. The face that grinned triumphantly above that gun had leered at him just so before, that day at the Sedalia rodeo. Lafe Turner's face. That time, that gun had spouted flame. He ran his tongue across his dry lips.

"Well, Turner?" His voice was steady. That fact surprised him; pleased him, too.

"Sit down. I want t' talk t' you . . . first!"

"You aim to kill me," Day said steadily. "That's it, isn't it?"

"Right!" Turner said crisply. "That's what I came here for."

Day nodded. "I'd—like to smoke a cigarette," he said.

"All right, light up. Only be careful how you move your hands! You smoke, I'll talk. It won't take long."

Day thrust two fingers into the pocket of his shirt and pulled a cigarette out carefully. His mind was a riot of disjointed thoughts. How had Turner tracked him here? He struck a match. One thought blazed suddenly across his mind. He stared across the flaming match.

"You called me *Elliott!*" he said.

The old man's cackling laughter slapped against the walls. "It's your name, ain't it? Gary Elliott. Son o' T. J. Elliott, the copper king. Only you're wonderin' how I found it out, eh, Elliott? . . . Sit down!"

Day lit his smoke and flipped the match toward the open door. He sat down stiffly in the proffered chair. "I'm—wonderin'," he said.

Turner came forward a step or two. There was no laughter now in his bleak face. His eyes seemed almost colorless and watery, but there was fire in them; an insane fire, Day thought.

"I loved that girl o' mine," Lafe Turner said. His voice was low, sing-song; the garrulous, thin voice of age. "Maybe she wa'n't all she ought t' been; she never had no mother to take care o' her. But she was all I had, and I loved her! And I hate you fer what you done t' her! I hate you most as much for makin' her unhappy and—desp'rit the way she was there toward the last as I do fer killin' her. . . . I got another reason fer hatin' you, too. Fer what you done t' Lary Day! Fer what you made me do, and Belle's friends, and them other honest folks: send a pore young man t' death when he was innocent. I hate you ten times over, Elliott, fer that!"

Day's fingers clutched convulsively upon the chair. "You know—that Day was innocent?" he breathed.

"I know it now! I know the whole rotten story *now*, Elliott! I know how you tricked my girl with yer wealth and yer lyin' promises, usin' a false name even then fer fear she'd get some holt on you. I even know how you got the idea o' layin' the blame for what you aimed t' do on Lary Day! You took Belle in yer car to a rodeo two weeks before the Sedalia one and you seen Day there. You seen how much he looked like you, and you laid yer plans accordin'ly! And it worked, Elliott; worked plumb perfect to the last detail! . . . But it was that same trip t' that rodeo with Belle that trapped you, finally!"

The old man paused. Day licked his lips. "Go on!" he said.

"Comin' back from that rodeo, you'd been drinkin' some and you got into a mixup with that big yeller car o' yers. It didn't amount t' much, but a traffic cop made you show yer papers t' prove you owned the car. Belle already knowed you then, so it didn't matter. . . . Only that cop took down yer name and yer automobile license number! And he remembers Belle. She smiled at him, he says. . . . And, when Sheriff Marsden come t' me the other day and hinted that they might be some mistake, or somethin', I remembered Belle's sayin' you'd had an accident that day, and we looked up that cop!"

Day's heart was pounding now. "So Marsden put you up to this!" he said.

The old man grinned. "Marsden aimed t' bring me back with him in his car, but I gave him the slip! Took a train ahead o' him. Hired a feller t' fetch me out here from Coronado. Yer Chink was real perlite t' me, but I had t' tie him up before you got here. I ain't a-gonna risk the law this time, you see. I'm gonna kill you, Elliott. I could-a done it when you first stepped in, but I wanted you should know what I've been tellin' you. How you slipped, and all. I wanted t' watch your face as I pumped lead in you!"

Lights flashed across the window at the old man's back and, dimly, Lary heard the racket of a car on the rough trail up to the house. He said, "The trouble is, my name ain't Elliott. It's Day. I'm Lary Day."

The old man grinned. "That game won't work both ways," he said. "In just about a minute now that clock behind you's gonna strike. And when it does—"

The racket of the car was louder now. The old man heard it, too, and crouched, his lips drawn back across his teeth. "Who's that?"

"I wouldn't know," Day said. "But I can prove—"

"Shut up!" The old man backed toward an inner door. A dark hall lay behind that opening. "I'll wait in here! But I'll have you covered, Elliott! Every second o' the time, I'll have a bead on you! One funny move—one word o' warnin' and I'll shoot! Don't think I won't! I ain't afraid o' what they'd do t' me. My life is finished anyway. And all the time I'm lookin' down the barrel o' this gun, I'll be seein' my little girl the way I seen her last—her head all smashed! I'll shoot, all right! Remember that!"

18

AS in a trance, Day watched Lafe Turner back deliberately into the hall. The darkness swallowed him. A clawlike hand reached back and drew the door shut after him. But not completely shut. A narrow crack remained, and through that opening Day caught the gleam of light reflected from the muzzle of the old man's gun.

Outside, a car's brakes squealed. A motor died. A car door slammed and heavy steps rang on the porch. Jason Northup's big voice echoed through the house.

"Hi, Lary! Come outside, man! You've got company!"

Day called, "Come in!"

The telephone rang startlingly, a long, shrill wail of sound. Day glanced at it but made no move to answer it. Northup's tall shape blocked the door. Day stood up then, his body tense, his nerves on edge.

"I've brought you a visitor, son." Northup's

face was wreathed in smiles. "It's a surprise!" He stepped aside and turned.

Day said, "Not Starr? Don't let her in!"

Northup chuckled. "It ain't Starr," he said.

A man came through the door and halted beside Northup. For an instant the newcomer's face was hidden by his arm as he removed his hat. He straightened then and grinned at Day.

"Howdy, son. Long time no see. Shake hands?"

The man was Blaine.

A cold paralysis held Lary motionless. Then suddenly he laughed. "Either way!" he said. "You've got me, either way—Sure, I'll shake hands with you. Come in! Pull up a chair!"

He laughed again. Blaine stared at him. His laughter sounded edged, unnatural, Blaine thought. But in Day's mind the grisly humor of the scene was paramount. *"If I'm Elliott,"* he thought, *"Turner's waiting to put a bullet in my back. And if I'm Day, here's Blaine to take me prisoner!"*

Northup closed in hastily and laid a hand on Lary's arm. "Steady, boy!" he said. "This ain't what you think it is. We're here to straighten out the mess you're in."

The telephone's shrill summons cut vibratingly across the following pause. Day turned instinctively and lifted the receiver down. "Hello!" A rasping voice came in along the wire. The crackling force of it was eloquent. Both Blaine and Northup turned to face the sound. They saw Day's posture change to one of frigid listening. "Say that again!" he snapped. "Go slow this time!"

Again the snapping crackle of the other voice. Day nodded now. "I've got it. Listen! Come through The Notch and ride up Pinto Creek. Got that? . . . Yes, Pinto Creek. Starr told me it was the first creek that dried up. I've got a hunch somebody's dammed it, back in the hills. That might account— . . . Okay. I'll be ahead of you."

The present situation had been jolted from his consciousness. But it came back to him. "That is, I'll be ahead of you if I can get away. I can't explain! Get goin', man!" The rasping voice came back at him in protest, but Lary slammed the receiver on its hook.

He whirled and shot a glance at the hall door. The baleful eye of Turner's gun glared back at him. He glanced at Blaine. Blaine, too, was watching him. Northup said, impatiently, "What's wrong?" and Day shrugged helplessly.

"Plenty! There's been a raid in Star Valley. Rustlers! They downed one of the MacGregor boys. Not dead, but badly hit. They want you, Doc. He was alone; ridin' back from town, Angus said. He just happened onto it. They got away with a big bunch, he thought. He just got home."

Northup nodded and reached for his hat. But he paused to shoot a glance from Blaine to Day. "Well? What you waitin' for?"

Blaine started guiltily. "Sure! Don't let me stop you, son. Maybe I can help? . . . But, hell, let's get this straight, first. I'm not arrestin' you. I've talked to Northup, here. He says you're innocent. I'm just about convinced of that myself. Didn't take much to convince me, really. Anyway, you've got grounds enough to get you a retrial. From what Doc says, I reckon we can dig up evidence next time to put the blame where it belongs. I hope so, sure."

Day stared at him. "I've *got* the evidence!" he said. "I've got the proof for *both* of you! For you, and for Turner!"

He laughed exultantly. Why hadn't he seen that before? Lafe Turner's evidence as proof to Blaine of Gary Elliott's guilt; Blaine's testimony on the other hand to prove to Turner Lary's true identity. The two things balanced; turned each of the horns of his dilemma in upon itself! He took a step toward the hall.

A shot cracked out and plaster spurted from the wall by Lary's head. He saw Blaine wheel, his right hand whipping up a naked gun. Behind the closed door to the hall, a man cried out. The cry choked off. The door burst open with a crash. Day caught a glimpse of Chang's bland face, distorted now; Chang, riding high on Turner's back, one arm around the old man's throat, the other holding Turner's gun aloft. The old man stumbled and went down. Another shot cracked out. A bullet ripped a splintery furrow in the floor. Day dived headlong for Turner's gun.

His left hand closed upon the weapon as he fell. He felt the hammer riding back as Turner tried to fire again; jammed his thumb into the gap between the hammer and the cylinder. Pain stabbed up through his arm as the firing pin drove deep into his flesh. He wrenched the weapon back and up. Turner yelped with pain as Lary forced his fingers back. The gun came free.

Chang stood up instantly and backed against the wall, arms crossed, his hands hidden in the sleeves, his face expressionless again. Day hauled Lafe Turner to his feet. "You fool!" he said. He was panting a little. Turner twisted desperately to free himself, but Day's grip held. His thumb was bleeding and his hand felt numb. "You doggone, peppery old fool!"

The old man writhed, still spitting oaths. Day said, "I ain't exactly blamin' you. Only, next time you get yourself all cocked and primed to kill someone, don't point yourself at me! I'm sick of it!"

Blaine laughed. The sound shocked all the anger out of Day. It stopped Lafe Turner's oaths. "By God!" Blaine said. "It's old man Turner on the prod again; He's right persistent, ain't he, Day? What's eatin' him this time?"

"His name ain't Day! It's Elliott!" Lafe Turner's voice shrilled up, saw-edged on Lary's jangled nerves. "Elliott, I tell you! Gary Elliott—the man that killed my girl!"

"Last time I saw you, you was sayin' it was Lary Day that killed your girl!" Blaine's voice was hard, accusing.

"But I was wrong! God, man, don't throw that up to me! Ain't I suffered enough? Ain't I? But this time I'm sure! I've got the proof!"

"Proof?" Blaine leaned forward a little, his eyes narrowing.

"Certain proof! Listen!" Turner's sing-song voice droned on, repeating almost word for word the story he had told to Day. "So now, you see? Young Day was innocent. This scallawag's a double murderer. He killed my girl and he's to blame for what we done t' Day."

A slow smile broke on Blaine's lean face. He met Day's eyes. "Congratulations, son!" he said, softly. "That clears you, sure!"

Lafe Turner screamed an oath. "You fool! Ain't I just been tellin' you—?"

Blaine raised his hand. "You tell him, Day."

"I've already told him," Day said slowly. "I'm not Elliott, Turner. I'm Lary Day."

The old man glared at him. "Don't lie! Day's dead!"

Day shook his head. "It was Elliott that was killed," he said patiently. "Look here." He ripped his shirt down off his chest. "Look, Turner. There's the scar of the slug you put into me in Sedalia that day. It's mixed up, sure; but what I'm tellin' you's the truth."

"It's true," Northup seconded him. "I'm a doctor and I've treated 'em both. I ought to know."

Chang spoke then for the first time since his stormy advent in the room. "It's tlue, all light," he said. "This man is not Gary Elliott. I know that plenty long time."

Day gasped and wheeled. Chang's sallow face remained expressionless but there was friendly humor in the narrow eyes. Day sat down heavily. "Oh, lord!" he gasped, and laughter welled up in him till it overflowed. "He knew; and you knew, Doc; and Starr—Who *did* I fool?"

Blaine grinned at Chang. "You came in handy, boy," he said. "Turner would just about've salivated the kid this time, except for you. What happened, anyway?"

"Ol' man locked me up," Chang said. "Mistake, though, to lock cook up in pantry. Knife having sharp point pushed lock back. Velly slow work, that. But I got out." He shrugged. "Easy after that, eh? Just jump on his back and glab gun."

"Sure!" Blaine said. "Just jump on his back and grab the gun. Easy! But dangerous. You'll do!"

"And in the meantime," Northup said, "that MacGregor boy is needin' me."

Day nodded and stood up. His gun still lay

where Turner had tossed it and he picked it up. "You go ahead. I'll fork a horse and head up Pinto Creek. I'm bettin' on my hunch."

He reached for the rifle that hung above the door. Blaine said, "Is this a private fight, or can I get in on it?"

"It's a free-for-all!" Day said. "Come on!"

They heard the doctor's car roar off as they ran down the hill toward the barns. Horses milled in the corral and Lary snatched a rope. He spoke to Blaine across the back of a wiry sorrel as he cinched the saddle into place.

"What brought you here?"

Blaine chuckled. "It's a long story, son," he said. "I'll tell you as we ride."

The night was oddly still. No breath of air moved in the underbrush as they climbed past the house and took the trail back through the hills; the trail Starr Landerson had shown to Day.

Blaine said, "Two days ago I got a letter from a man named Vale. Not a friend of yours exactly, I gather, this Vale. He spilled the dirt. Told me about your accident and about this amnesia thing. He said you had the general public fooled, but he was wise to you. He says you sure ain't Gary Elliott."

Day nodded. "Vale saw me ride a buckin' horse," he said. "That's how he knew."

"Well, Vale figures if you ain't Elliott you must be *you*. Which ain't such lousy figurin', at that! I plumb agreed with him. But then, I asks myself, who was the man I killed? So I took a little run down to Wigwam Gap. Right at first, Danny Lightfoot no sabe white man's talk worth a damn. But when he saw that I was wise, he opened up. I had most of it right there; enough to convince me that you never killed that girl. Elliott had to be the guilty one, else why'd he come so readily to Pop Greer's call? . . . That eased my mind, I'm tellin' you! There was a time there when I thought I'd killed the wrong damn man! Not that I felt so *good* when I thought I'd killed *you!* But killin' an innocent bystander, so t' speak—That *would* have been too bad!"

Lary laughed quietly. "That's a bit mixed up in spots, but I get the general sense of it."

Blaine grunted. "Anyway, I drove on down here to take a look-see. I'd met Northup once and Vale said Northup was treatin' you, so I just dropped in on the Doc. You'd just left, he said. We drove on out and Northup did some talkin' on the way. That brings us up to date."

Day nodded. "I figure Vale's the man we're after now; or one of them." He filled the gaps until Blaine's knowledge of the situation was complete. They had reached the bed of Pinto Creek and headed west.

Blaine said, "What's this, now, hunch you're workin' on?"

"Just this: Pinto Creek was one of the strongest tributaries emptyin' into Sweetwater, but it was the first one to dry up when the drought closed down. That might've happened naturally, or somebody might've damned the creek back in the hills. If a man had a bunch of stolen stock hid out—and what Pop said would indicate that there *was* stock hidden in the hills —he might be smart enough to dam a creek to make sure he'd have water for 'em, mightn't he? Then, what with the drought and the cattle he'd got usin' the water, there'd be no overflow and the creek would dry up. . . . Anyway, that's the way I figure it."

They rode in silence after that, following the steep waterway in its tortuous course cut deep into the stair-step benches of the Antelopes. It was slow work. Their way ran now and then along short stretches of sandy gravel where the stream had followed some more gentle slope, but oftener it led between high darkening walls among thick, water-rounded rocks on which the horses' feet slid dangerously and struck fire. Time and again they were forced to retrace their steps and leave the creek to skirt some obstacle, but always they returned to it. The hours passed. A moon, surrounded by a misty veil, climbed over them, and slid ahead to drop at last beyond the peaks.

Blaine halted once and dismounted to hold a match beneath his hat while he searched a sandy bit of ground. "No tracks," he grumbled wearily. "Your hunch don't look so good to me."

But Day led on. "It's the only hunch I've got," he said. "And the lack of tracks don't prove it's wrong. If I'm right, they'd have an easier way in than this, that's a cinch. But this is the only way I know of findin' it, if this *is* a way."

At dawn, they rode between close, towering walls that shot up dizzily on either side until they seemed to meet and blend. Day shivered suddenly and laughed. "I hope the damn dam holds, providin' there is a dam!" he said. "I'd hate to meet a wall of water comin' through this place!"

But the high walls fell away precipitously as they passed the ridge through which the stream had cut, and Day drew rein abruptly when a barrier of crosswise logs loomed up ahead of them. Blaine stared at it and shed his weariness.

"So you were right!" he said.

Day nodded and swung left, up the steep bank, around the barrier. Logs, wedged crosswise in the channel of the stream, had formed a wall against which brush and rubble had been piled to choke the waterway and, back of it, a shallow lake lay, mirrorlike, against a gentle slope. Grey morning light fell across the peaks to show cattle moving on that slope in numbers that astonished Day. And, to the left, where pinon pine made a dark blotch against the shoreline of the lake, a red bull's-eye of fire sent a slow spiral of white smoke toward the sky.

Day whistled softly as he turned to Blaine. "Two thousand head, at least, along the slope!" he said. "And one man guardin' them, there by the fire."

"More comin', though," Blaine said.

Far to the right, a thin black line moved slowly past a shoulder of the astern ridge and curved lazily along the slope toward the lake.

Muted by distance, Lary heard the strident echo of men's voices raised in cowboy yells. Down by the fire, a man stood up and stepped aside a bit to stare toward the sound. Day wheeled and spurred the sorrel to the left, around the southern shoreline of the lake. Blaine followed him. They rode in shadow from the eastern ridge, their hoofbeats muffled on the sandy turf. But as they turned back north again around the lake, Day slowed his sorrel to a walk.

A rich voice carrying the strain of an old Negro spiritual came to them through the pines ahead, growing stronger as they neared the fire until the words, "Swing Low, Sweet Chariot," rolled up in golden melody. They came almost within the firelight glow before they paused and stepped down into the grass. A fat man squatted by a cooking fire, his back to them. Beyond the fire, a brush lean-to made shelter for a heap of gear; bed-rolls and camp supplies. The song broke off abruptly and the singer turned. His face was black. White eyes rolled up at them. The man lunged and whirled.

"Just take it easy, Sam," Day said. His friendly tone relieved the black man's fright.

The Negro halted, poised for flight. "I got no gun," he said.

"Make sure of that," Day said, and Blaine stepped forward, running swift dexterous hands along the black man's sides. He stepped back then and shook his head. Day grinned. "You just tend to your cookin' then. That ought to look real natural—to them."

And so it was a peaceful scene into which Red Vale and Ladd and Travis and Dupree rode noisily just as the sun began to touch the higher peaks. Behind the shed, Day touched Blaine's arm. "The redhead's Vale," he said. "He's bad. Or so I've heard."

He stepped out then and walked toward the fire. Blaine followed him. Out of the corner of his eye, Day saw that Blaine was drifting left, away from him. Day held his rifle well ahead of him, the hammer back. He heard the clear metallic click as Blaine's spur touched a rock. Vale whirled.

The scene held so while seconds passed. Ladd turned, saw Vale's tense pose, and glanced at Day. Dupree and Travis got their warning from the Negro's face. They wheeled and froze.

Blaine's steady voice was low, unstressed.

"We've got you covered, gents," he said. "We're nervous, though. Don't startle us! . . . Put up your hands."

19

IT flashed through Lary's mind that there was anticlimax here. This victory had come too easily.

But Ladd's shot smashed that illusion into bits. Ladd had reached the fire ahead of the other three and had squatted down to lift a pot of coffee from the coals. He was behind the others now, so that their bodies shielded him. His gun flame lanced between Joe Travis' legs. Day saw Blaine reel and drop his gun. And, in that moment of uncertainty, Day faced the four of them.

Dupree spat out an oath as his right hand shot down toward his holstered gun. Vale wheeled and dived among the milling mounts. That movement brought Day face to face with Ladd. Ladd's gun was high, kicked upward by its own recoil. Ladd chopped it down.

Day crouched and fired. The rifle's whip-like crack was lost in the deep thunder of the forty-fives. Dupree was firing now, and Vale. Day glimpsed Vale's arm above a horse's back and pumped a shot at it. A horse reared crazily and lunged away. Lead snicked Day's hat. But Ladd was down. *That* shot had scored.

Dupree spun crazily and clutched his arm. The rifle in Day's hands felt hot. Joe Travis stood motionless, his mouth agape. The thing had happened while a man might count to three, quick-time. "But what's the matter with Dupree?" Day thought. "I never shot at him!"

The guns fell silent sharply. Hoofs beat a sharp tattoo as the outlaw's horses lunged away. And Blaine walked slowly into Lary's line of sight, a forty-five held loosely in a bloody hand.

Day gulped to fill his aching lungs. So it had been Blaine who had shot Dupree! And Day had thought that Blaine was dead!

Blaine spoke in an aside to Day, still watching Travis and Dupree. "Get Vale!" he snapped. "Don't let him get away!"

Day turned. He had lost track of Vale, but now he saw a man swing up astride a running horse far up the slope. Vale must have ridden Indian-style, along the horse's side, until now. Day knelt and brought the rifle up. Three shots streaked up the slope before the gun missed fire. Day thought, "It's empty, and I missed!" But then he saw Vale's horse swerve drunkenly and pitch headlong. Vale's body made a grotesque, sprawling flight. He fell and rolled and then was still.

Day reached far back along his belt and slid fresh cartridges out of their loops. His ears were pounding with a rhythmic beat which he did not identify. He kept his eyes upon those two dark blotches where Red Vale and a horse lay sprawled against the russet carpeting. The final shell slid home. He threw the lever down and back again. Vale lurched up then and Lary brought the gun to aim.

"No need to shoot," Blaine said. "Those jaspers will attend to him."

Blaine's warning turned Day's gaze toward the south. And there he found the source of that deep pounding that had filled his ears. A pack of horsemen swept up through the trees and split, part angling up the slope toward Vale, the others swinging down toward the fire. Day saw Vale run a staggering step or two, then turn and lift his hands.

"It's the MacGregor boys," Day said. He stood up wearily and let the rifle fall into the cradle of his arm.

"I hoped it was!" Blaine said. "I've heard

'em comin' since before the fight. . . . You all right, son?"

"All right," Day said. "But you? I thought—"

"I'm hard to kill!" Blaine said, and grinned. "That first shot hit my rifle; smashed it back against my ribs like the kick of a mule! It knocked me down and splinters from the bullet cut my hand a bit. That's all. It put you in a hot spot, though. You sure stood up to 'em!"

Three men came down toward them now and Lary leaned his rifle up against the shack. Four other men were bringing Red Vale in. Vale could not be very badly hurt, Day thought. He walked unaided, limping a little.

Angus MacGregor swung down heavily and frowned at Day. "You all right, lad? I had strict orders to look out fer ye! . . . Losh, mon. Ye're hit! There in the leg!"

Day stooped. His right knee ached and there was blood in a dark smear above his boot. He remembered now that he had felt a stab of pain as he dropped down upon that knee to fire at Vale. But, bending now, he saw the cause of it. A jagged rock thrust up through inch-deep dust that blanketed the ground around the shack and he had knelt on that. He laughed.

"There's the bullet that wounded me," he said. "It's just a scratch—"

His voice broke off abruptly and he did not rise. The rock was tinged with blood where his right knee had struck and, just ahead and to the left of it, he saw the print of his left boot.

Day's mind flashed back to that bright morning after Pop Greer's death. He saw again that narrow ledge below the mesa's rim where Pop Greer's murderer had knelt to fire those first two shots. There, too, had been the prints of a man's boot and of his knee. But those prints had shown the imprint of a man's *right* boot and of a man's *left* knee!

Day straightened slowly. A group of men surrounded Blaine. Another group held guns upon the prisoners. Someone was binding up Dupree's smashed arm. Day met MacGregor's anxious gaze.

"I've just found out," he said, "who killed Pop Greer!" Out of the corner of his eye, Day saw a figure detach itself from the group around the prisoners and move to join the men surrounding Blaine. A man near Blaine said, "Howdy, Lem. You fellers ought t' meet. Blaine, want you t' meet Lem Marsden. Lem's the sheriff here."

Day said, "Marsden!" very low.

MacGregor said, "He came with us. Seems the telephone operator listened in when I called you. I didn't know that Marsden had got back. But the telephone lassie passed the word t' him. He met us just below The Notch."

Day nodded. "That makes it—nice!" he said.

He turned and faced the group surrounding Blaine. His face was set in tense, hard lines.

"Marsden!"

This time his voice cut through the buzz of talk, keen, challenging. Men turned to stare at him. He saw Lem Marsden standing next to Blaine. He called again.

"You, Marsden! I want to talk to you!"

His voice betrayed his purpose, seemingly, for men stepped back to clear a space. Across a dozen empty yards, Lem Marsden stared at him.

"All right. I'm listenin'!"

Day said, "I've been real dumb. A fact's been starin' me square in the face for days and I've been blind. But now I see! . . . You're heeled, Marsden. So am I. So make the most of it! . . . You killed Pop Greer!"

A silence fell in which the strained, harsh

breathing of the listeners was audible. Lem Marsden's eyes were startled now.

"Pop Greer?" he said.

Day's tight-lipped grin was not a pleasant thing. "The man who rode down after you the night you shot at me out at the Broken Bar!"

Marsden's eyes flicked right and left as if he sought an opening for escape. His voice was high and edged. "You're crazy, Elliott! I wasn't at the Broken Bar that night! I took the train—"

"I know," Day said. "And you had witnesses! You played it safe! But that train slows down almost to a stop before it crosses that bridge just west of town. I saw that happen twice, myself, and didn't figure what it meant. But I do now! You jumped off the train there, Marsden. You had a car waitin' near that bridge and you parked it again just off the road below the Broken Bar. . . . You started out of Coronado by train, Marsden; but you hit San Francisco in a car! Lafe Turner told me *that*. . . . You're trapped! Go for your gun!"

"Wait, son!" Blaine's shout cut stridently across the hush, too late.

Day saw Lem Marsden's left hand jerk and dart inside his open vest. His own hand seemed to move without command, not hastily, but up and forward in a smooth, clean arc. He felt detached, entirely calm. There was no fear in him. The thing was preordained and absolute. It struck him as poetic justice that Greer's training should equip him to avenge Greer's death. He felt the gun recoil and drop; recoil again. He lowered it.

Lem Marsden's shot came after that, belated, unaimed. It struck the lake and rose in screaming ricochet. That sound was still in Lary's ears when Marsden fell. He turned and held out his gun, butt-foremost, to Blaine.

Blaine shoved it back. "Don't be a fool!" he said.

Day sheathed the gun. Two men were bending over Marsden now and one of them looked up at Day. "He's dyin', Elliott. He wants to talk to you."

Day walked deliberately to stand beside the fallen man. "How—did you know?" Lem Marsden asked.

"When I knelt to fire at Vale," Day said, "I hit my knee against a rock. My *right* knee, see? You knelt to fire at me, that night. We found your tracks, next day. But—you're left-handed,

Marsden. The tracks we found were made by a left-handed man!"

Blaine said, "I'm pretty dumb, I guess. But how'd you figure that?"

Day said, "How would *you* kneel to fire a rifle, Blaine?"

Blaine stared at him, then balanced an imaginary rifle in his hands and knelt. Day said, "You see? Your right knee on the ground, your left foot flat, ahead of it. But Marsden didn't kneel like that. He put his *left* knee down, his *right* foot flat. He'd hold a rifle opposite to what you would, you see."

Blaine said, "That's right!" and stood erect.

"It's true enough." Marsden's voice was weaker now. "I—killed him. No use denyin' it. Not hard—t' prove it, I reckon, now you know where t' look. Folks must've—missed me, on the train. Folks seen me—drivin' through. Them things—wouldn't've mattered, though, unless somebody had a cause—t' seek 'em out. I thought the alibi—"

He shrugged. "I lose. But you—" He grinned at Day, "*You* lose, too! Lafe Turner will—see to that!"

He coughed and shuddered violently. Day would have answered him, but Marsden's eye swung now to Blaine. He gasped, "You—officer of the law—get—Randall! He—hired me t' do that job! He—cheated me! By God, I'll take him—down with me!"

He grinned triumphantly as he fell back. Day turned away.

Even in their repetition, as Blaine repeated them that night, his voice softened by the quiet friendly peace of Starr's big living room, those words with which Lem Marsden died held a vindictiveness, a strange disloyalty, that sickened Day. Starr sat beside him there, and Northup faced them from an easy chair across the room. A door stood open to afford a glimpse of Tom McElvey's room. There were two invalids there now, both doing well. Blaine sat beside a table in the center of the bigger room, his lean brown face etched out in sharp relief as he stared at the fire and talked.

For it was cool that night. A strange, chill wind had grown in the northwest that afternoon and thick blue clouds had swallowed up the sun before its time. Riding down out of the hills against that wind, Angus MacGregor had bewailed an aching tooth. "Cold wind and clouds," he said, "and now me tooth! Three likely signs o' rain, I'm thinkin', men!" And now, beside the fire, he rubbed his jaw.

"I have na doot," he said, "Brett Randall's heard them words by now. And, if I know the mon, he'll run. There's no convictin' him, o' course; but we'll be shed o' him."

Blaine nodded. A moment later he glanced aside at Day. "After you left," he said, "we found that Marsden wore a bandage underneath his shirt; a gunshot wound grazed his side."

Day said, "So Pop had put his mark on him, just like he said!"

A silence fell, and finally MacGregor spoke again, less solemnly. "There's an amazin' lot o' cows up there," he said reflectively. "Some strays, but mostly branded with the Star. That's na bad news, eh, Starr? There's many a dollar that'll soon come rollin' home t' ye."

Northup chuckled. "There speaks the Scot! But how d'you reckon Vale expected to get rid of them?"

Blaine said, "I asked him that. At first, of course, the plan was for Elliott to dispose of them, after he'd took legal title to the other stock. But then, when Elliott lost his memory—!" Blaine grinned. "Vale saw a chance to cash in on his own account. He said he had a buyer down in Mexico. He aimed to make this one more raid and then get out."

The talk was dwindling now. Day felt the pressure of Starr's fingers on his arm. He closed his eyes. This room was warm with friendliness, he thought. He felt at ease, filled with a sweet, enduring peace. Conflict was over now, and stress. All questions answered . . . except one.

He said, "Blaine, what's the penalty for forgery?"

Blaine grinned. "What name'd you sign?"

"Why, Gary Elliott's. I told you that. A check, you know, and that bill of sale to Starr."

Starr said, "That needn't worry you. I haven't cashed that check. I'll tear it up." She smiled at him. "I knew, you see, that you weren't Gary Elliott. I held the check for fear it might make trouble for you, afterward."

He said, "You're sweet! But, still, we've got to spoil that land transfer, somehow. That mine—"

"Oh, what's a mine or two?" Blaine said. "It's all inside the family—or am I wrong? You're marrin' him, ain't you, Miss Starr?"

"That's right!" Starr said.

"She's marryin' *me*," Day said. "Not Gary

Elliott! And, as it stands, the mine's in Elliott's name."

Blaine reached out suddenly and laid a hand on Larry's knee. "Wait, son," he said. "There's somethin' I've been tryin' t' get told all day. I'm glad I waited, now. This is the time for it. You better brace yourself!" He smiled.

Day stared at him. Some inner sense forewarned him of a shock and he stood up.

Blaine said, "Doc Northup, what was T. J. Elliott's first wife's name? Her maiden name?"

Across the silence in that room, Day turned to meet the doctor's kindly eyes. "I would've told you sooner, Lary, if I'd known." Northup's voice was oddly vibrant. "I didn't know until last night. Blaine asked me then. We looked it up on an old deed. Her name was Lorna, son. . . . Lorna Winslow Day."

Day caught his breath. He felt Starr close to him and groped for her. Her arm around him steadied him. There was no sound. Outside, the wind had died.

"You're—sure?"

"I'm sure," Blaine said. "You see, I liked you, son. You remember that story you told me while we was stopped there at Apache Tanks that day? It stuck with me. I thought I'd killed you, see? That story haunted me. . . . I went to San Francisco after that to get a prisoner. Down there, I thought I'd look it up. I searched the records, son. It's there, all right, just like she said it was. Her name, and T. J. Elliott's; the date, and all. . . . Your name is Elliott, you see. You're Lary Elliott. That mine—the Broken Bar—the Elliott estate, is yours."

Day did not speak. He turned and took Star Landerson into his arms.

THE END